FIREFIGHTER PEGASUS

FIRE & RESCUE SHIFTERS 2

ZOE CHANT

Copyright Zoe Chant 2016
All Rights Reserved

❦ Created with Vellum

The Fire & Rescue Shifters series

Firefighter Dragon
Firefighter Pegasus
Firefighter Griffin
Firefighter Sea Dragon
The Master Shark's Mate
Firefighter Unicorn

All books in the Fire & Rescue Shifters series are standalone romances, each focusing on a new couple, with no cliff-hangers. They can be read in any order. However, characters from previous books reappear in later stories, so reading in series order is recommended for maximum enjoyment.

CHAPTER 1

Connie West was an excellent navigator. She could find her way through a fog bank at thirty thousand feet with nothing more than an altimeter and a compass. She could plot a course across three states with just a paper map, and beat pilots flying planes with the latest GPS computers. She could navigate back to an unfamiliar landing field at night with nothing more than her own two eyes.

And she could also, unfortunately, always find her way to the roughest, dirtiest gambling den in any city in the world. She'd had a lot of practice at *that* one.

She'd never been to the English seaside city of Brighton before, but it only took her an hour of searching its narrow back streets before she found the sort of bar she was looking for. She knew she'd come to the right place by the way the room fell absolutely silent the moment she opened the door.

The only patrons in the place were a small group of hard-eyed men, their glasses frozen halfway to their mouths. Connie flinched as their suspicious stares assessed every inch of her ample body.

As one, the bar patrons seemed to silently conclude that a lone, plump, nervous-looking young woman in khakis and a flight jacket was unlikely to be an undercover cop. The low buzz of muttered conversations resumed as the men turned back to their drinks and cards.

Breathing a sigh of relief, Connie edged her way to the bar. "Excuse me? Sir?"

"Well, you certainly aren't from around here." The shaven-headed bartender didn't look up from the shot glasses he was cleaning, if that was the right word for what he was doing with his gray, greasy dishcloth. "I think you've taken a wrong turn, Yankee girl."

"I'm looking for someone." Connie showed him the well-worn photo she always carried with her. "Very tall, very loud, very Irish?"

The bartender's eyes flicked from the photo to her face momentarily. "No idea."

Connie fumbled through the unfamiliar bills in her wallet, pulling out a twenty. "You sure about that?"

The bartender gave her a long, thoughtful look. Connie put the twenty down on the bar, keeping her finger on it.

With a shrug, the bartender jerked his head in the direction of a door at the back of the bar. "You could try in there. Though if I were you, I'd go straight back home instead."

Connie sighed. "Boy, do I wish I could."

Leaving the money on the bar, she headed for indicated door. It opened into a narrow, dirty stairway that sloped steeply down into darkness. As Connie gingerly descended, a familiar Irish voice floated up the stairs.

"—the most beautiful plane you'll ever have the pleasure of laying eyes on, my hand to God. If you won't take my word for it then you can all come and see her in action at the race next week. In fact, would any of you fine gentlemen care for a little side bet...?"

"Not again," Connie groaned. She hastened down the last few steps so fast she ran straight into the door at the bottom.

"What was that?" said a man sharply.

The door opened, and an enormous hand grabbed Connie's shoulder. She stumbled as she was yanked forward into a small, smoky room.

A small group of men were seated around a green-topped table, cards and cigarettes in their hands. They started at Connie's intrusion, their cards reflexively jerking closer to their chests.

All except one man. *He* greeted her arrival with a dazzling smile—and not the slightest hint of repentance.

"Darlin'!" Connie's dad exclaimed with evident delight.

The huge man holding Connie's shoulder brandished her in her father's general direction. "This yours, West?"

"You'll not be speaking of my daughter like that, thank you," her dad said indignantly. "Or else I'll be having to ask you to step outside."

Connie twisted her shoulder free from the giant. "Dad, you *promised*!"

"Ah, now, don't be like that." Connie's dad flung his arms wide, regardless of the other men's scowls. "It's just a friendly little game."

Connie looked at the not inconsiderable pile of money already stacked in the center of the table. Even with her unfamiliarity with British currency, she could recognize they were mostly high-value bills. "A friendly game? Dad, you know we can't afford this right now!"

One of the other men at the table folded his cards, casting a level look over them at Connie's dad. "Is that so?"

"I said I'd be good for it, and I will be." Her dad gestured extravagantly at her. "With my lovely daughter copiloting my plane with me, we're a dead cert for winning the air race next week. The prize money is as good as in my pocket."

"It is *not*," hissed Connie. She cast a weak, apologetic smile around at the seated men. "We really have to go now. Sorry for any misunderstanding."

"But I'm winning!" her dad protested as she tried to tug him to his feet.

"Yeah, you can't go yet, West," said a man whose skinny, supple fingers seemed oddly out of proportion with the rest of his hands. Connie mentally nicknamed him Longfingers. "Have to give us a chance to win back our money."

"That's only fair," said another man.

A general rumble of agreement ran around the table. There was an ominous undertone to the sound that made Connie think of a pack of wolves, growling low in their throats as they closed in on their prey.

No matter how infuriatingly impulsive Connie's dad was, at least he wasn't stupid. "Ah, well," he said, starting to gather bills toward him. "Better call it a night. Sorry, lads."

Longfingers caught his sleeve. "No. You said you'd play, so you play to the end."

Connie's hand closed on the pepper spray she always carried in her pocket. It wouldn't be the first time she'd had to use it to buy them a quick escape.

Connie's dad flashed his trademark disarming, charming smile as he brushed off the man's clinging fingers. "I wish I could, my friend, but I daren't cross my daughter here. No man can change her course when she's got the bit between her teeth. Women, eh?"

Out of the corner of her eye, she noticed the giant man cast a swift, questioning glance at Longfingers. The smaller man jerked his chin in an almost imperceptible nod.

"He's been cheating," the giant announced. "I saw him. He's got cards up his sleeve."

"Now, no one likes a poor loser—" Connie's dad started.

A large man to his right grabbed his wrist, twisting it viciously. Connie's dad's protests fell on deaf ears as the thug ripped back his jacket sleeve.

A card fluttered out, landing softly on the tabletop. The black ace stared up like an accusing eye.

Connie's dad's mouth hung open for a moment. "I honestly don't know how that got there," he said weakly.

"Cheat!" roared the thug.

"*Dad!*" yelled Connie.

"Run, Connie!" Her dad ducked the first punch, toppling off his chair. "*Run!*"

The table overturned as men shot to their feet, shouting and pushing. Cards flurried into the air. Her dad disappeared into the middle of a mob of angry muscle.

Connie took aim and maced the nearest man. He screeched, dropping his cigarette to claw at his eyes. But that still left five, and her action hadn't gone unnoticed.

"Don't get in the way," growled the giant. "Ain't none of your business."

Connie tried to get him with her pepper spray, but he was too fast for her. The giant shoved her aside, kicking her feet out from under her with a casual movement. Leaving her sprawled on the ground, he waded into the fight.

Pushing herself up to her hands and knees, Connie saw her dad for moment between the angry, shoving bodies. Most of the men were just taking outraged, imprecise swings at him, but not the giant. *He moved with complete control, cutting through the crowd like a shark through water.*

Connie's blood ran cold. In a flash, she knew her dad had been set up. And she had a bone-deep certainty that he was in terrible danger.

She desperately cast around for some way to distract the mob. Her eye fell on her dropped pepper spray... and the still-lit cigarette beside it.

I can't believe I'm doing this, but...

Connie grabbed the cigarette and a handful of fallen bills. She'd never wondered how well money would burn, but the answer turned out to be 'surprisingly fast.' Connie yelped, involuntarily dropping the bills as flames licked at her fingers. They landed in a puddle of spilled alcohol and cards.

The result was considerably more impressive than she'd intended.

"Fire," Connie yelled, as loud as she could. *"Fire!"*

"What?"

"Where?"

"Hey, there *is* a fire!"

Longfingers glanced back over his shoulder. His face froze as he noticed the flames. Even though the fire wasn't *that* big yet, he suddenly looked utterly terrified.

"Oh no," he moaned. "Hammer!"

"What?" The giant's head appeared above the crowd. His expression changed to horror too as he saw the fire. "Oh, *shit.*"

The other men had lost interest in Connie's dad by now, more concerned with rescuing their money before it was caught by the rapidly-spreading flames. The giant hesitated, one meaty hand still wrapped around her dad's throat. "What about—?"

"We'll finish the job outside!" Longfingers was already bolting for the door. "Come on, we gotta get out of here! Before *they* come!"

"No!" Connie threw herself in their path. She grabbed for her dad's dangling legs, trying to wrestle his limp body away from the giant. "*No!*"

"Out of the way, girl," the giant snarled.

Connie didn't even see his fist coming. The last thing she heard as darkness closed over her was the fire's greedy, triumphant roar.

CHAPTER 2

Chase Tiernach barreled gleefully at sixty miles per hour the wrong way down a twenty mph street. He lived for this—the thrill of speed, the urgency of the mission, the horrified looks on other drivers' faces as they found themselves unexpectedly confronted by a wall of bright red steel hurtling toward them.

His inner pegasus shared his elation. Driving wasn't as good as flying, but it still made his stallion prance and snort with fierce joy. Like all pegasi, his stallion was intensely competitive. There was nothing that gave it as much satisfaction as matching speed and strength against a rival, and *winning*.

To Chase's delight, an oncoming Lexus convertible tried to play chicken with twenty tons of oncoming truck. Whooping, Chase slammed the accelerator to the floor. The truck roared like an animal. Chase laughed out loud as the sports car was forced to veer off the street, ruining its shiny chrome hubcaps.

"Bastard!" the Lexus driver yelled.

Chase gave him a cheery wave out the side window as he hurtled past. "Just doing my job!"

"Alpha unit checking in," Commander Ash said calmly into the radio. The Fire Commander balanced easily in the passenger seat, barely swaying despite the fire truck's wild, bouncing motion. "Any update on the situation?"

"Observers say there's a lot of smoke," Griff's voice crackled out of the speaker. Concern thickened the dispatcher's Scottish accent. "The buildings around are close-packed, and not in good repair. High danger of the fire spreading."

"Alpha unit ETA three minutes," Ash said. "Currently proceeding east down Montgomery Street."

"Correction!" Chase spun the wheel. "Currently proceeding north up Stewart Street!"

"Please note correction," Commander Ash said into the radio. He gave Chase a level look. "Chase, *why* are we proceeding north up Stewart Street?"

"I can get us there in a minute this way," Chase yelled over the sing-song wail of the fire truck's siren. "Trust me!"

"Just when I thought I couldn't get any more nervous," muttered Hugh. The paramedic was strapped in behind Ash, and had a death-grip on his safety restraints. "Chase, are you *sure* you can get to Green Street this way?"

"Positive." Chase threaded the fire truck neatly through a slalom course of parked cars. "Up here, then nip down that little alley, and we'll pop out in just the right place."

"What little alley?" Hugh's face went nearly as white as his hair. "Chase, that's a pedestrian cut-through!"

"It's fine. There's no one in it." Chase knew that for a fact—his pegasus gave him an innate sense of where people were. It was what let him drive so fast in perfect confidence.

Ash eyed the rapidly approaching alleyway. His eyebrows drew together slightly, just the tiniest crack in his otherwise unflappable expression. "We will not fit."

"Yes we will!" Chase gunned the accelerator.

There was a horrible crunching sound.

"Mostly!" Chase added.

"Alpha Team proceeding east down Green Street," Commander Ash said into the radio. "Without side mirrors."

"May I ask if we are there yet?" John Doe said plaintively from his seat next to Hugh.

In the rear-view mirror, Chase could see that John had his eyes tightly closed. He was faintly green, which was not a good combination with his long, indigo hair.

Chase stomped on the brake, spinning the steering wheel at the same time. The fire truck lurched on two wheels, sliding sideways round the corner as it decelerated. The smell of burning rubber from the truck's tires mixed with the thicker tang of smoke.

"And here we are," Chase announced brightly.

Ash had the side door open even before the truck had fully come to a halt. He jumped down with a smooth, practiced leap. The rest of the fire team disembarked more slowly as Ash's intense, dark eyes swept the scene.

To Chase, it all just looked a mess. Thick black smoke was billowing out of the door of a shabby bar, while a small crowd milled uncertainly on the opposite side of the road. From the clouded windows, it looked like the entire building was filled with smoke. A man was collapsed on the sidewalk out front, but no one seemed to want to go to his aid.

Chase couldn't even begin to guess where the fire had started, or the best way to go about putting it out. His talents were suited to making instinctive, split-second decisions when driving, not to this sort of tactical stuff.

Fortunately, that wasn't his job.

Commander Ash gave the building the barest glance before turning back to his fire team. "Basement. There must have been a great deal of paper debris."

That was the advantage of being led by the Phoenix. He always knew *exactly* where the fire was.

"I am keeping the fire from spreading further, but we must work quickly," Ash continued. He had the slightly abstracted look that meant he was focusing on using his special talent to control the flames. "Hugh, attend to the casualties. Chase, is there anyone in the building?"

Chase concentrated. His stallion raised its head, sniffing the wind. Its ears pricked up sharply. There *was* a scent under the smoke. Something compelling, and familiar...

Chase shivered, suddenly feeling oddly on edge. "Yes. One person. A woman, I think."

"In which case, John and I will go in." Ash looked up at the enormous shifter. None of the fire team were small men, but John still loomed over them all. "We will need respiratory gear."

John nodded, heading back to the truck to unpack the breathing masks. Normally, they didn't need such equipment—Dai, their fire dragon shifter and the last member of the team, would have just strolled straight into the smoke without any protective gear at all. But he was off duty today, and miles away in London with his mate. The fire team would have to carry out the rescue the old-fashioned way... and just hope that they could reach the trapped woman in time.

Chase stared into the swirling smoke darkening the windows of the bar.

Why do I really, really wish that Dai was here right now?

"Chase. *Chase.*" He started, Commander Ash's voice finally getting through to him. "I said, get the hose ready."

"What? Oh." Chase shook himself, forcing himself to concentrate on the job instead of his strange, rising sense of urgency. "Right."

He tried to turn toward the truck, but his stallion reared up and *screamed* at him. His pegasus was frantic, hooves flashing and wings beating with agitation.

Run! Go! Now!

And abruptly Chase knew exactly who was trapped in the burning building.

"*Chase!*" Ash's shout followed him as he plunged into the smoke.

Immediately, Chase's eyes started to burn. He closed them, relying on his stallion to guide him as he charged blindly through the bar. He could feel the heat of the floor even through the thick soles of his boots.

Commander Ash's telepathic voice abruptly crashed into his head. *What are you DOING?*

Trust me! Chase sent back.

He couldn't spare the time to explain further. All of his concentration was focused on sound and touch, tiny cues that told him how to navigate safely through the burning building.

His lungs burned in his chest, but he didn't dare draw in a breath. He could taste how thick the smoke was, bitter and acrid on his tongue. Even a single lungful would put him helpless on the floor, coughing his guts out.

Holding his breath, he charged down a flight of stairs, leaping the ones that had already fallen in. Embers swirled around him. His uniform jacket and trousers protected him from most of them, but some still burned the bare skin of his neck and face. Chase barely felt the pain. His stallion danced in agitation, urging him on.

There. There!

Chase scooped her up, cradling her protectively against his chest. There was no time to check whether she was breathing. His own lungs were burning, every instinct in his body desperate to draw in air. White spots danced behind his closed eyes as he blindly raced back up the stairs.

His chest felt like he was being squeezed by iron bands. Chase stumbled, strength draining out of his legs as his body cried out to breathe. Only the weight in his arms kept him moving forward. His entire world narrowed to the single desperate need to get his precious burden to safety.

Just one more step. Just one more. One more—

He stumbled out into light and cool air. Chase collapsed to his knees, still cradling her tightly in his arms. Clean air had never tasted so good. For a moment, all he could do was blink his streaming eyes, and breathe.

Ash seized him under the arms. The phoenix shifter dragged both Chase and the woman he'd rescued further away from the burning building. "Hugh!" he shouted.

A second later, Chase felt Hugh's bare hand on his neck. A familiar, comforting warmth spread out from the paramedic's touch. The pain from his burns eased as Hugh's healing talent took effect.

"I'm okay," Chase said, jerking away. "Concentrate on *her*. Please, now!"

Hugh shot him a curious look, but transferred his focus to the rescued woman instead. Chase watched anxiously as the paramedic ran his bare hands over her throat and face. She was pale and motionless, limp in Chase's arms. Terror filled him, as thick and deadly as smoke in his lungs.

When she finally took a breath, all the air rushed out of him. He sagged in relief.

"That's it," he said to her, stroking her singed red hair back from her beautiful face. "There you are. There you are at last."

"Chase. Explain yourself." Chase had never heard Ash so coldly furious. A faint heat-haze shimmered in the air around his shoulders, in the shape of burning wings. "What is going on here?"

"Commander Ash, allow me to introduce Constance West." Chase never took his eyes off Connie's face. A broad grin spread across his own face as she started to stir. "That's it. You're okay, Connie. Everything's going to be okay."

Connie's eyelids fluttered open. She looked straight up at Chase. Her eyes widened with recognition.

"Oh, *no*," she croaked, and promptly fainted again.

Chase beamed up at the rest of the fire team. "She's my mate."

CHAPTER 3

*C*onnie drifted up into consciousness to the reassuring sound of beeping equipment. A faint scent of roses mingled oddly with a stronger smell of disinfectant.

Hospital. I'm in a hospital. I think.

How did I get here?

She had a confused, dreamlike memory of being pulled out of a burning building. But she must have been hallucinating from smoke inhalation, because she could have sworn she'd been rescued by—

"Hello, Connie," said an impossible, Irish voice.

Connie opened her dry, scratchy eyes, blinking. The vague blur of color next to her bedside resolved into an instantly familiar, infuriatingly handsome figure. The ghost from her past grinned down at her, as cocky and charismatic as ever.

Connie groaned aloud, closing her eyes again. "Chase Tiernach, *go away.*"

"All right," Chase said, unexpectedly.

Connie reopened one suspicious eye. She couldn't see him anymore.

"Is this better?" Chase inquired solicitously from the foot of the bed.

"I mean go away entirely. Out of my room. Out of my life. Again." Connie sank lower down in the bed, pulling the sheets over her head as if she could hide from her past under the covers. "What are you even doing here?"

"The rest of my team had the fire well under control and didn't really need me any more, so my Commander very kindly agreed that I should accompany you in the ambulance." The mattress dipped as Chase sat down on the edge of the bed.

She was acutely aware of the warmth of his hip through the bedclothes. "What?" she said blankly.

She felt him shrug. "Well, actually, I didn't bother to ask him until we'd arrived at the hospital, and his response was more along the lines of 'Chase, it is a very good thing you are already five miles away from me,' but I think that counts as agreement, don't you?"

"None of that," Connie mumbled into her sheet, "made the slightest bit of sense."

"How about this, then." Chase shifted on the bed. Even without looking, Connie knew he was leaning over earnestly, his brilliant, lying black eyes full of sincerity. "I've missed you desperately. I'm overjoyed to find you again. Will you marry me?"

Connie pushed herself up on her elbows to stare at him in disbelief. "Are you completely out of your—"

She stopped mid-sentence as more of her surroundings came into focus. Every flat surface in the small private room was covered in roses. For a moment she had a mad thought that perhaps Chase had bribed the paramedics to bring her to a florist rather than a hospital. It was exactly the sort of thing he'd do.

Chase himself was set off by a background of glorious white roses that made the perfect contrast to his dark good looks. His shoulders were broader than she remembered. His long, muscled arms bore unfamiliar scars, the barely-visible traces of old burns. Instead of a custom-made designer suit, he wore a smoke-stained fire-resistant uniform. His thick black hair, once so carefully cut and styled, was now tousled and singed.

But his face was exactly the same, unchanged even after three years.

She should know. Despite her best efforts, that face had haunted her dreams every night.

Connie tore herself away from those bright, compelling eyes. *Remember what he did,* she reminded herself. *He's a lying, womanizing cheater.*

Don't fall for him again.

"Okay," she said firmly. "First things first: No. I am absolutely not marrying you."

Chase's hopeful expression fell. "So you're still mad at me."

"I caught you naked in bed with two other women, Chase!"

On the night I'd finally decided to sleep with you, Connie didn't add aloud. Chase didn't need to know *that* little detail.

She glared at him. "Of course I'm still mad at you."

"But you never even gave me a chance to explain," Chase said, so rapidly that his strong Irish accent made his words run together. "You see, I went to the club for a drink, and the next thing I knew-"

"I wasn't interested in excuses then, and I'm definitely not interested now," Connie interrupted. She pushed the old hurt back down into the bottom of her heart. "It was a long time ago, anyway. It doesn't matter anymore."

"Yes, it *does*," Chase insisted. "Please, Connie. You have to believe me, I never meant to hurt you. I don't even know what happened!"

"I said I'm not interested." Connie rubbed at the bridge of her nose, feeling the start of the familiar headache that prolonged exposure to Chase tended to inspire. "Why are you wearing a firefighter's uniform? Why is this room full of roses?"

Chase spread his quick, agile hands. "The room is full of roses because you like roses. I'm wearing a firefighter's uniform because I'm a firefighter."

None of *that* made any sense, either, but Connie let it go as a far more urgent question finally occurred to her.

She sat bolt upright in the bed, panic seizing her. *"Where is my dad?"*

"He's fine," Chase said, and Connie's heart started beating again. "We found him outside the bar. He's been pretty badly roughed up, but he'll be okay. He's here in the hospital, too."

"I have to see him." Connie threw back the sheet, struggling to her feet. "Take me to him, now!"

Chase caught her as she swayed. His gaze flicked downward. Connie belatedly realized that she was wearing nothing except a backless hospital gown. *Literally* nothing.

"Here." Chase shrugged out of his firefighter jacket, offering it to her. His lips quirked teasingly. "Not that I don't like what you're wearing…"

With what dignity she could muster, Connie put the jacket on over the hospital gown. It was streaked with soot and reeked of smoke, but it was better than wandering the corridors bare-assed. She pulled it closed around her ample hips as best she could. "Thanks. Now take me to my dad."

~

"Dad!" Forgetting her own aches and bruises, Connie rushed to his bedside.

Connie's dad gave her a pale shadow of his usual wide grin. "Hello, pumpkin. We've both had better days, eh?"

She would have squeezed his hand, but both his arms were encased in plaster casts and suspended in traction. "Are you okay? How did you get away from those goons?"

"Ah, once they broke my arms, they lost interest." Despite his light-hearted tone, Connie could tell that he was deeply upset. "Connie, I was trying to get back in to you, I swear. But they kicked me in the head as they ran away, and I couldn't get up, and—"

"Shh. I know, Dad. It's okay." She sat down on the chair next to his bed. "You'd never have left me."

"It's all my fault." Her dad blinked rapidly, his eyes suspiciously damp. Connie pretended not to notice. "The nurses said you were all right, though?"

"I'm fine." It was, surprisingly, true. For someone who'd been unconscious in a burning building, Connie felt pretty good. "I was lucky. I guess the firefighters managed to get me out before I breathed in too much smoke."

Chase, who was hanging back in the doorway, made a small, choked sound, like a hastily stifled laugh.

Her dad's gaze moved to him. For a moment, he just stared blankly... and then his jaw dropped. "Good God. That's never young Tiernach, is it?"

"It's good to see you again, Mr. West," Chase said, coming forward. His black eyes danced. "Just to let you know, I still haven't crashed. Well, at least not a plane."

"You are still the most god-awful student I've ever had the misfortune of teaching to fly," her dad informed him. His brow creased. "What in the name of all that's holy are you doing wearing a firefighter's uniform?"

"Why do people keep asking me that?" Chase said to the ceiling.

"Apparently, he's playing at being a firefighter," Connie said to her dad. "Don't ask me why."

"I am not *playing*," Chase said indignantly. "I happen to be a very respected and valuable member of my crew. Just ask..." He trailed off, apparently searching for a name. "Hmm. Actually, perhaps it would be best if you didn't."

"Chase Tiernach, a productive member of society. Now I really have seen it all." Connie's dad shook his head. "Well, if you did rescue my daughter, I'm eternally in your debt, sir."

"Excellent!" Chase said brightly. "In that case, may I ask for your blessing?"

Connie's dad looked across at her in a wordless request for interpretation.

"Ignore him," Connie said firmly. "He's leaving now, anyway."

"Oh, I don't have to be anywhere else," Chase assured her. "I already told Commander Ash that I'm taking an indefinite leave of absence. He thought it was an excellent idea." He paused, a slightly worried expression briefly flashing across his face. "I *think* I still have a job. Though I might have to persuade him on that point, later."

Connie glared at Chase. "My dad needs peace and quiet to recover. He doesn't need you. *I* don't need you. Go *away*, Chase."

Her dad shifted uneasily, despite his broken arms. "Ah. Well. I hate to say it, but there might actually be something he could help us with."

Connie threw up her hands. "Dad! Don't encourage him!"

"I can be *excessively* helpful," Chase assured him earnestly. "What do you need?"

Her dad cleared his throat. "You know the big air race next week, over at Shoreham Airfield?"

"The Rydon Cup? Of course!" Chase's eyes brightened. "I've been looking forward to it ever since they announced it was going to be flown here this year."

"We were going to enter our plane. Me flying, Connie navigating— we were sure to win. But now..." Her dad made a helpless little motion with his head, indicating his broken arms. "I, ah, was kind of counting on winning that race."

"We're not going to ask the Tiernachs for money, dad," Connie said sharply. "Don't worry about the race. We'll just have to pull out. Things will be a little tight, but I'll manage."

Already she was making mental lists of air shows where she could display her plane, places she could advertise for passengers, evening jobs she could take… It wouldn't be the first time she'd had to hustle to cover her dad's debts. No doubt it wouldn't be the last.

It's not a disaster. I can get us through this. I always have.

Her dad dropped his head. "It's about more than the prize money," he mumbled.

With a sinking sensation of dread, Connie recognized that guilty, hangdog expression. "Dad, *what did you do?*"

Her dad's eyes shifted from side to side, as if seeking an escape route. "You know the money we used to transport the plane here from America?" he said reluctantly.

"So *that's* where you were," Chase said. He scowled. "I have to sack my private detectives. Apparently they've been chasing wild geese all over Europe."

He hired private detectives to find me?

Connie brushed away the thought. There were more important things to deal with right now.

"You didn't want to tell me where the money came from, so I assumed you won it gambling," she said to her dad.

"I did! In... a manner of speaking." He fidgeted. "I just haven't *quite* won the bet yet."

Connie groaned, burying her face in her hands. "Let me guess. You bet that you could win the Rydon Cup."

"It was a sure thing!" her dad protested. "Hardly a gamble at all! More like a, a loan. And we did need the money to get out of the country right away."

"Oh?" Chase said, cocking his head to one side with interest.

"He got deported," Connie said grimly. "My mom was American, so I'm a U.S. citizen, but he isn't. Let's just say that in future, *I'm* handling all his immigration paperwork. Not to mention our taxes." She sighed. "Okay, Dad. How much do you owe *this* time?"

Her dad avoided her eyes. "Well...I didn't really bet money, as such. Sammy wasn't interested in that."

"Sammy?" Connie sucked in her breath. "Not Sammy Smiles. Dad, tell me you didn't make another deal with him. Not after last time."

"Sammy Smiles?" Chase said, his eyebrows shooting up. "The shark?"

"How on earth do you know Sammy Smiles?" Connie said, momentarily distracted. She couldn't imagine that Chase, the son of a billionaire, had ever had need of a loan shark.

"We move in some of the same social circles, shall we say." All the good humor had slid away from Chase's expression, leaving him looking uncharacteristically grim. "He's pretty notorious. Well, that explains why you're lying there with two broken arms, Mr. West."

"I knew his reputation, but I thought..." Connie's dad trailed off, hanging his head in shame again.

He thought he could talk his way out. He always *thinks he can talk his way out.*

Connie shook her head in despair. "Dad. What deal did you cut with Sammy Smiles?"

"He offered money. A lot of money. Enough to pay for our move. Tickets, shipping the plane, an apartment, everything. And all I had to do was win the Rydon Cup, and he'd write off the entire debt." Her dad peered up at her sidelong. "It *was* a good deal, Connie."

Cold dread closed around Connie's heart like a fist. "And if you lost?"

Her dad swallowed hard. "Then he got our plane."

Connie was struck literally speechless. She stared at her dad, overcome by the sheer scale of the betrayal.

"Wait," Chase said, looking from one to the other. "*The* plane? Connie's plane? You gambled *Connie's airplane?*"

"Technically it's half my plane," Connie's dad said defensively. "And it *was* a sure thing."

Chase looked like he would have loved to break Connie's dad's arms himself. He took three quick, agitated paces back and forth, running his hands through his hair as though physically unable to keep still. Connie still couldn't move, frozen in disbelief.

The plane. He gambled my mother's *airplane. The only thing we have left of her, and he staked it in a* bet.

"Right," Chase said, swinging round. There was a determined set to his jaw that Connie had never seen before. "I'm going to fix this. Mr. West, I'm going to need to talk to Sammy. I presume you've met him?"

"Yes, I met him in the Marina a few days ago," Connie's dad said. He was looking at Chase with the sort of hopeful, ingratiating expression he usually turned on Connie when he wanted *her* to clean up his messes for him. "He's in town for the race. I think he's staying on his yacht, though. Do you think you'll be able to find him?"

"If he's within my range," Chase said, mysteriously. He stared at her dad in an oddly intent way. "Can you describe him for me? And the men who attacked you, too."

"Well, they were about—" Connie's dad began.

"That'll do," Chase interrupted, his smile reappearing. "Yes, I can find them. Connie, don't worry. Everything's going to be fine."

"No it won't," Connie said numbly. She gestured at her dad. "Sammy Smiles wants my plane badly enough to do *this*. There's no way he'll listen to you."

"Oh, I think he will," Chase said, flashing a grin that was rather more feral than usual. "I can be *very* persuasive."

CHAPTER 4

"Why did I let you talk me into this?" Griff shouted into Chase's ear.

Chase snorted. *You've been sitting behind a desk for too long. You said you wanted to get out into the fresh air.*

"I didn't say I wanted to fall into fresh air!" Griff clung onto Chase's mane for dear life. "Do you have to go so high?"

High? This isn't high! He beat his wings harder. *Look, you can still see the boats on the water below.*

Chase felt Griff's weight shift on his back as the dispatcher peered down.

They're those tiny little specks, Chase pointed out helpfully.

Griff let out a low moan, burying his face again in Chase's neck. "Oh, this was a bad idea."

You're afraid of heights? Really? Chase let out a whinny of laugher. *You can't be afraid of heights! You're half eagle shifter!*

"And no doubt I wouldn't be afraid of heights," Griff snarled, his knees squeezing Chase's flanks hard enough to bruise, "if I could actually shift!"

I've always wondered about that. Chase curved his neck to look back at Griff thoughtfully. *Maybe you just need proper motivation?*

"Chase, you bastard, don't you daaaaaaare—!"

Griff's last word turned into a drawn-out yell as Chase folded his wings, arrowing down out of the sky. Chase was tempted to do a barrel roll, just to see what other interesting noises the dispatcher might make, but there wasn't time for horsing around. A long, sleek white yacht cut through the waves below, and Chase's pegasus senses told him that their quarry was aboard.

A couple of crew members looked up as he soared overhead, pointing out his black-winged shape to each other. They had to be shifters; no ordinary human could see a mythic shifter who didn't want to be noticed. But unfortunately, Chase's 'don't see me' mind trick didn't work on other shifters, not even those who turned into ordinary animals rather than legendary beasts.

Well, he hadn't counted on having the element of surprise. Chase beat his wings, landing neatly on the raised deck at the rear of the superyacht.

Griff slid off Chase's back. He pushed his wind-swept, tawny hair back from his face, eying the crew members who were rapidly converging on them.

"I hope you know what you're doing, Chase," he muttered.

Chase shifted back to human form. "Trust me."

"This is private property," a uniformed crew member yelled at them. From the man's thick neck and beefy arms, Chase was pretty sure his role on board wasn't just to serve drinks. "You need to leave!"

Chase flashed the thug his most dazzling smile, along with his firefighter badge. As a mythic shifter, his clothes and any small items in his pockets came with him when he shifted, which came in handy for situations like this. "We're here to see Sammy Smiles. Official business."

The thug paused at the sight of the metal shield. "Uh..."

Chase flipped the leather wallet shut before the man could realize it wasn't actually a police badge. "I suggest you fetch him right away."

The thug dithered for a moment, then snapped his fingers at a smaller man. "Go get the boss."

Well? Chase sent silently to Griff as the crew member ran off.

Griff's piercing golden eyes swept the ring of men surrounding them. Even though he couldn't shift, he still had an eagle shifter's ability to see tiny details that others would miss.

"Mako sharks, mostly," Griff murmured. "The big one is a tiger shark."

Chase's smile widened. *No one in our league, then.*

Griff shot him a sidelong, exasperated look. "Will you at least *try* not to tempt fate?"

"Now, I'm fairly certain I would have heard about a pegasus shifter joining the police," said a new voice, sounding amused. The crowd of shark shifters parted to let the speaker through. "So I'm guessing Chase Tiernach has dropped by for a visit."

What was that about tempting fate? Chase sent to Griff.

Sammy Smiles towered a good foot over both of them. His bald head seemed to slope directly into his wide shoulders, which were as thickly muscled as a body-builder's. He was not so much clothed as upholstered in a brilliant white suit.

His wide smile showed way, *way* too many teeth.

"Well now," drawled the Great White shark shifter in a strong Texan accent. "No fires here, boys. Aren't you a little out of your jurisdiction?"

Chase matched his shit-eating grin with one of his own. "I'm here on behalf of a friend. Shane West."

"Ah, good old West. Great pilot. Great gambler, too." Sammy's brilliant smile didn't touch his flat, cold eyes. "I'm so looking forward to seeing him fly in the Rydon Cup in a few days. Should be quite the race."

"Sadly not," Chase said lightly. "Seeing as he has two broken arms."

"Really." Sammy's expression didn't change. "What a pity."

Chase held the shark shifter's stare. "Naturally that means all bets are off."

Sammy sighed regretfully, his teeth sharp and gleaming. "Ah, no can do, boys. I've got my reputation to consider. West bet me his plane, and, well, a deal's a deal."

"Do you cheat on a deal?" Chase countered. "Because I know for a fact you were responsible for landing West in hospital."

Sammy's smile never wavered. "That's a mighty rude accusation, son. Folks could take offence."

Chase raised an eyebrow. "Are you claiming you knew nothing about it?"

Sammy spread his stubby-fingered hands. "Nothing whatsoever."

"Lying," Griff said, very softly.

Sammy looked at the dispatcher, his smile turning just a shade less friendly. "Excuse me?"

"I'm sorry, I should have introduced you," said Chase. "This is Griff MacCormick. Have you heard of the MacCormicks? They're a Highland eagle clan. They are remarkably good at spotting things. Prey. Body language. Lies. That sort of thing."

"We know that two of your people started that bar fight," Griff said. "And that bar fight turned into a fire. And *that* puts it under the jurisdiction of Commander Ash."

"You may have heard of him," Chase added.

"The Phoenix," Sammy said. His smile was still fixed in place, though it was looking more and more like a predator baring its teeth rather than any sort of human gesture. "Well now, that's all mighty fine, but I have to say I don't know why you think my boys were involved in any bar fight. Let alone a fire."

Chase gazed contemplatively up at the clear blue sky. "There's an interesting legend about pegasus shifters. Says that we were created by Hermes, the God of Messengers. Do you know what a messenger needs to be able to do, above all else?"

"Fly real fast away from bad situations?" suggested Sammy.

Chase looked the shark shifter straight in his black, dead eyes. "Find people."

"West saw his attackers," Griff said. "Chase picked their faces right out of West's mind. And so he knows they're right here on this boat, right now."

"Still claim you know nothing about the attack, Sammy?" asked Chase.

Sammy held Chase's stare for a long, long moment.

Then the shark shifter tilted his head. "Rusty," he said to one of his henchmen. "Ask Hammer and Eights to step up here, would you?"

I told you this would work, Chase sent psychically to Griff, as the henchman disappeared off below decks.

"Don't count your chickens too early," Griff muttered grimly. "Or your sharks. He's up to something."

A few uncomfortable minutes passed, during which Sammy and Chase continued to smile at each other. Chase's jaw was starting to ache by the time the henchman hurried back, escorting two other men.

"Hammerhead and... octopus, I think," Griff informed Chase under his breath.

He didn't have to point out which was which. The hammerhead shark shifter was nearly as big as Sammy, while the octopus shifter had uncannily long, supple fingers. Both looked incredibly edgy.

"Pay attention, Mr. Eagle," Sammy said to Griff. He switched his attention to his two fidgeting thugs. "Boys, you remember I mentioned a certain Mr. West the other day?"

"Yes boss," rumbled the hammerhead shifter.

"What exactly did I say?" Sammy asked, glancing over at Griff.

The octopus shifter twined his hands together nervously. "That he was such a good pilot, the only way he'd lose the Rydon Cup was if he broke both his arms."

"Did I *tell* you to break both his arms?" Sammy pressed.

Both shifters shook their heads.

"Was I, in fact, laughing and smiling in such a way that might indicate I was just joking around?"

The hammerhead and the octopus shifter nodded silently.

Sammy swung back to Griff. "Seems to me that my boys had what you might call an excess of initiative. A bit of high spirits that just got a little out of hand. Don't you agree, Mr. Eagle?"

Griff mouth set in a thin line. "He's telling the truth. As far as it goes."

Damn! Chase thought. He maintained his smile, though it took all his willpower. He wasn't going to give the shark shifter the satisfaction of seeing him wrong-footed.

Sammy put his hands in his suit pockets, rocking a little on his heels as he contemplated his cowering henchmen. "Now, boys, from what these nice folks tell me, the Phoenix is very upset about that fire."

"It wasn't us!" the octopus shifter blurted out.

"It was the girl," said the hammerhead. "She started it."

"Yeah." The octopus shifter nodded vigorously. "If the Phoenix is gonna burn anyone, it should be her."

"Thank you, Hammer, Eights." Sammy dismissed them with a flick of his hand, and they scuttled off gratefully.

"Don't you worry, boys," Sammy said, turning back to Chase and Griff. "I'll make sure my men learn a real good lesson from this little incident. It won't be happening again in future, you have my word. Thank you for bringing the matter to my attention, and please do give the Phoenix my very *warmest* regards."

"But what about the plane?" Chase's mind raced frantically. "What about the bet?"

Sammy shrugged. "West already took my money. I intend to collect the payment."

"I'll pay the money back myself," Chase said, his fists clenching. "Double. Triple. Whatever you want, just name your price."

"Now, that's a mighty fine offer. I know your family has deep pockets. But, see, here's the thing." Sammy gestured around at his luxurious yacht. "So do I. Keep your money, boy. I don't want it. But I *do* want that plane for my collection. And I intend to have it."

"Wait!" Chase called, as the shark shifter started to stroll away. "You can't take Connie's plane!"

"If West's plane doesn't win the Rydon Cup, then it's mine," Sammy said over his shoulder. "That was the bet."

Chase paused.

If the plane *doesn't win...?*

He threw back his head and laughed, long and loud. Griff stared at him as if he'd started barking. Sammy paused mid-step.

"Oh, Sammy." Chase chuckled. "You have no idea how glad I am you said that."

Sammy turned around again, folding his arms across his broad chest. "And why might that be, son?"

"You just said that the bet is on the plane, not the pilot." Chase grinned at him. "West's plane *is* going to race. I'm going to fly it."

Sammy's eyes narrowed. He didn't otherwise move, but the group of shark shifters surrounding Chase and Griff started to circle them, drifting closer.

"And if you think West is good," Chase added, "you should see *me* fly."

"Now why," Sammy said softly, as the circle of shark shifters closed in like a trap, "do you think you're going to be flying anywhere? This is the open sea, boys. You're a long way from the Phoenix, or the Parliament of Shifters, or any of your dry-lander laws. We have our own rules out here. And you two are *way* out of your depth."

Chase's grin widened. "Funny you should say that."

The yacht tipped to one side as a massive, scaled head erupted from the water. Sammy's shark shifters scattered in panic as a long, sinuous neck arched into the air, dwarfing the boat. Seawater streamed from indigo scales, falling like rain onto the yacht's deck.

"I think that you'll agree that *he* is very much *not* out of his depth," Griff murmured.

Sammy lost all traces of his smile at last. "Ah," he said, looking up.

"That," Chase said conversationally, "is the Walker-Above-Waves, Emissary to the Land from the Pearl Throne, Oath-Sworn Seeker of the Emperor-in-Absence, Anointed Knight-Poet of the First Water, and... you know, it's so tricky to remember all these titles. What was the last one, Griff?"

"Firefighter for the East Sussex Fire and Rescue Service," Griff supplied, grinning himself.

"Oh, yes, that was it." Chase turned back to Sammy, who had gone as pale as his suit. "His real name is a little tricky to pronounce above water, so we just call him John Doe. Say hello, John."

The sea dragon rumbled, with a sound like continents colliding. The shadow of his great, fanged head fell over the shark shifter.

"So you see, Sammy, I *will* be flying West's plane in the race," Chase said. "And I'm going to *win*."

CHAPTER 5

Connie stared numbly out of the bedroom window of her cheap rented apartment. From up here, she could just about make out the colored lights of Shoreham Airfield. Even in the dark, she knew exactly which speck of light marked the location of the small hanger that housed her plane.

Her *mother's* plane.

Connie had only been twelve when her mom died. But she remembered her mother's strong hands, wrapped over hers on the handle of a wrench, showing her how to disassemble a wheel assembly. She remembered the comforting smell of engine oil mingling with her mother's floral perfume. She remembered her mother's delighted laugh when a repair went well, and her inventive cursing when it didn't.

And she had a distant, dreamlike memory of being very small, small enough to curl on her mother's lap as she worked on restoring the plane's controls. Small enough to be perfectly happy, cocooned in the cockpit with her mom, utterly secure and safe. Because mom could fix *anything*.

"I wish you were here, mom," Connie said softly to the distant, hidden plane.

She drew in a deep breath, scrubbing the back of her hand across her face. There was no time for tears. For a long time now, she'd had to be the one who fixed things. She would fix this now.

She wouldn't let anyone touch her plane.

Chase's head appeared, upside down, at the top of the open window. "Good news!" he announced cheerfully. "I'm going to fly your plane!"

Connie leaped backward with a strangled yelp. "Chase, what are you *doing?*"

"Hanging by my knees from the guttering." He flashed her an inverted grin. "It was the fastest way down from the roof."

Connie rubbed her forehead. "Do I even want to know what you were doing on the roof?"

His devil-may-care smile faltered. "Probably, but that's one of those things I'm not allowed to talk about. Sorry."

Oh. One of those *things.*

She'd frequently run into *those things* with Chase, during the brief summer they'd spent together three years ago. There had been certain topics that made him go uncharacteristically silent if they came up in conversation. Some of them were silly, innocuous things, like his favorite type of animal or why his whole family seemed to treat his desire to fly airplanes as somehow perverse.

But there were more significant things he wouldn't discuss either. Things like why a rich playboy who was notorious for countless flings with supermodels would abruptly become obsessed with the plain, dumpy daughter of his flight instructor. Things like why he'd pursued her so relentlessly, despite her initial refusals. Things like why someone like Chase would want someone like her.

Compared to *that*, his habit of turning up on rooftops seemed positively normal.

Connie knew from experience that questioning him further would only result in him doing something astonishingly random, and usually quite dangerous, in order to force a change of subject. "If I don't let you in, you're going to hang there all night, aren't you."

Chase's trademark grin reappeared. "How well you know me, my love."

"I'm not your love." Nonetheless, she stood back from the window, gesturing him in.

Chase flipped himself neatly through the window, landing on his feet. Connie's heart, which was still hammering after the shock of his abrupt appearance, gave an odd little skip. He'd changed out of his firefighter uniform into black jeans and a slim-cut button-down shirt, sleeves rolled up to show off his tanned forearms. The neck of the shirt hung open a little, displaying the strong lines of his throat and a hint of muscled chest.

Remember. Remember all the things he is. Womanizing, dishonest, fickle, flighty, unreliable...

Unfortunately, there was one other thing that he undeniably was: *Gorgeous.*

Connie folded her arms, trying to conceal the traitorous rise of her hormones by giving Chase a withering glare. "Why are you here, Chase?"

"I told you." Chase plopped himself down her bed, lounging back against the headboard and looking infuriatingly at home. "I'm going to fly your plane."

Connie stared at him. "No, you most definitely are not."

Chase spread his hands, palm up. "Well, if you want I could co-pilot while you fly it, but to be honest I think we've got better chances the other way round. You're a much better navigator than I am, after all. I haven't had a lot of experience in doing that sort of thing. And I bet you've been studying the race course for at least a month already—"

"*Chase,*" Connie cut across the babble. "Start at the beginning. What on earth are you talking about?"

"I talked to Sammy. He wouldn't drop the bet entirely, but I made him stick to the literal words of the agreement he made with your dad." Chase's white teeth flashed in his feral smile. "The bet's on the plane, not specifically on your dad flying it, you see. So now everything will be fine. We just have to win the Rydon Cup together, flying your plane."

Shoving Chase's feet out of the way, Connie sat down heavily on the end of the bed. "We *just* have to win the Rydon Cup. Right. One question. Are you completely insane?"

"What?" Chase looked wounded. "You know how I fly."

"Like God Himself gave you the wings of an eagle," Connie said through gritted teeth. "And the brains of a hummingbird."

"That's the nicest thing you've ever said to me," Chase said, grinning. "Well? Come on, Connie. You and me. We can do it. Together."

Connie pinched the bridge of her nose, thinking it over. Much as every fiber of her being screamed *NOOOOOO!* at the thought of Chase even sitting in her mother's plane, let alone flinging it across the sky, she had to admit that he *was* a ridiculously fast pilot. Not a *good* one—he was far too cavalier about little things like 'air traffic control' and 'the ground' for that—but she'd be sitting right behind him in the co-pilot's cockpit. She'd be able to take over control if he got too reckless.

Maybe they really could do this together.

"All right," she said reluctantly. "It's a terrible, crazy, ridiculous idea. But I don't have a better one. Are you up to date with your license? How often do you fly?"

Chase's mouth quirked. "You'd be surprised. But the type of piloting you mean... pretty frequently. I fly the service helicopter when we need air support putting out fires. And I've got a plane of my own that I try to take up on a regular basis. Every week or so, usually."

Connie eyed him suspiciously, but couldn't tell if he was lying. "I'm surprised you find time, what with the firefighting as well."

Chase's eyes darkened, his expression turning uncharacteristically serious. "Whenever I flew, it made me feel closer to you. Knowing that you were up in the same sky, even if I didn't know where."

I am not *going to fall for him.*

"Well, I'm glad to hear you've been practicing," Connie said, determinedly ignoring his intense gaze. "We'll go up in the plane together tomorrow. I'll teach you the quirks of the controls. I warn you, it won't be like anything you've ever flown before."

A quick, private look of amusement flashed across Chase's face. "I think you'll find I'm a fast learner."

"I know you are. When you actually decide to listen." She jabbed his muscular leg with her finger. "I'm serious, Chase. If you're going to get behind the controls of my mother's plane, then you'd better be serious, too."

"When it comes to you," Chase said, all traces of laughter sliding away, "I am *entirely* serious."

The heat in his dark, intent eyes made an answering warmth spread through her. It was like he was a magnet, pulling the compass of her soul out of alignment. She knew, *knew,* that he was a cheating playboy, and yet she couldn't help but want to throw caution away and fly straight into his arms.

She stood up abruptly. "Good. In that case, I'll see you tomorrow. Good night, Chase."

He remained sprawled across her bed.

"I said, *good night*, Chase." She glared at him. "That means it's time for you to leave. Now."

"Ah, well." Chase folded his arms comfortably behind his head. "I'm afraid I can't do that."

Connie rolled her eyes. "Chase, you live in this city. There is no possible way you are going to convince me that you don't have somewhere to go."

"I do. A very nice place. Much nicer than this, if you don't mind me saying so." He sat up, swinging his feet off the bed. "In fact, why don't we go back there now? I'd like to show you my roof garden. You can sit in the hot tub and look out at the sea, and—"

"I am *not* going anywhere with you. And you are leaving. Now."

"I really, really can't," Chase said firmly. "Considering that Sammy Smiles has already put your father in hospital, I can't take the risk of leaving you alone."

Connie folded her arms across her chest. "I can take care of myself."

Chase's jaw set. "I mean it, Connie. I'm not leaving your side."

"And I'm not having you *staying* at my side every moment until the race," Connie retorted.

Chase's roguish grin flashed again. "Good. Because actually, I'm planning on sticking with you for a lot longer than that. Something like forever."

Connie threw up her hands in despair. "Look, if I have sex with you, will you finally agree to just leave me alone?"

The words slipped out from her unbidden, fuelled by a combination of exasperation and attraction. She hadn't meant to say it.

But it did mean she had the pleasure of finally seeing Chase Tiernach completely, utterly, and absolutely lost for words.

"Well?" Emboldened by his stunned silence, Connie took three steps back toward him, planting herself right between his knees. "Come on, Chase. You and me, right here, right now. Get it out of your system, so you can finally get over me."

So I can finally get over you.

Chase swallowed, hard. "Connie, we... please don't tease me. You don't understand what you mean to me."

"I'm not teasing." Throwing common sense to the wind, Connie ran her fingertips up Chase's bare forearm, tracing the rock-hard swells of his muscles. "Don't tell me a playboy like you doesn't always carry around a condom or two."

"Actually, I don't." Chase said hoarsely. "So—"

"Well, I'm on birth control anyway, so as long as you'll take my word for it, it's not really a problem. In your line of work I assume you have to have a clean bill of health, right?"

Chase couldn't have looked more stunned if she'd walloped him across the back of the head with a two by four. "Yes, of course, but.... you can't actually be serious?"

"Why not? We're both consenting adults. There's unfinished business between us, so lets finish it, for once and for all." Connie started undoing the buttons of her top. "Then we can both move on with our lives."

Chase's hand closed around her wrist, stopping her mid-motion.

Connie could feel the contained strength in the grip. He was shaking, ever so slightly, as if it was taking immense force of will to hold himself back.

It felt *wonderful* to make someone else be the sensible one for once.

"Don't do that," he said, something dark and primal roughening his voice. "Not unless you really mean it."

Connie met his black, heat-filled eyes, and discovered that she really *did*.

"This is a one-time offer, Chase," she said. "Take it or leave it."

With a low moan, Chase pulled her down to him. The last vestiges of Connie's better judgment burned away at the first touch of his lips on hers. Chase kissed her desperately, as if she was the air he needed to breathe. Connie kissed him back with equal fervor, three years' worth of pent-up desire finally bursting free.

Chase's hands skimmed her thighs and hips, exploring her curves. Connie abruptly needed to feel those agile, sensitive hands on her bare skin. Breaking the kiss, she tugged her top over her head in one swift, impatient movement.

Chase's breath hissed between his teeth. His arms tensed, holding her away from him so that his hungry gaze could devour her, savoring every curve of her exposed body.

Then he actually closed his eyes.

"Connie," he said hoarsely. "If you want me to take this slowly, I'm going to need a second."

"You've never in your entire life taken *anything* slowly." Connie tried to press closer to him, but his rigid arms were like iron bars. "And for God's sake, Chase, don't start now!"

Chase let out a sound that was half-laugh, half-growl. Then, before Connie had even registered the movement, he had her bra off. She gasped as his mouth closed fiercely over one breast, even as his hands flashed downward to undo the button of her jeans. She closed her eyes, surrendering herself to the glorious sensation of Chase's tongue flicking and circling her nipple.

Chase yanked down her jeans and panties. He made a low, feral sound, deep in his throat, as his strong fingers grasped her butt. Then, somehow, she was on her back on the bed, the last of her clothes falling away. Chase's agile hands and expert mouth seemed to be everywhere at once—teasing her nipples, sucking at her neck, exploring her wet, eager folds.

"Oh," she gasped, as his long fingers slid into her. "*Oh.*"

She threw back her head, fiery pleasure sparking through her. His mouth was hot on her breasts, his teeth nipping at her skin with barely-contained passion. She wound her limbs around him, her hands tangling in his shirt, his jeans rough against her bare legs as climax overtook her.

"More," she demanded, when she could speak again. She tugged at his shirt, desperate for his body naked on her, in her. "Now, Chase!"

She felt his lips curve against her breast. Then he was gone, the air suddenly cold on her flushed, sweaty skin. She propped herself up on her elbows to watch greedily as he unbuttoned his shirt.

Though they'd briefly dated, all those years ago, she'd never let him get this far before. Now she was finding out what she'd been missing.

Her breath caught at the sight of his broad chest and lithe abdomen as he pulled off his shirt. Every muscle in his body was sharply defined, shaped and honed to perfection by the tough, physical nature of his job.

Chase bent over to strip off his jeans, revealing his slim hips and tight ass. Then he straightened, turning.

"Holy shit," Connie couldn't help yelping.

He was hung like a fucking *horse*.

From the quick, pained smile he flashed her, she guessed she wasn't the first woman to have second thoughts when confronted with his frankly intimidating erection.

"Do you want to stop?" he said, his voice shaking with raw desire. The swollen head of his enormous cock was already glistening with eagerness.

Connie very nearly said "Yes," but her body had its own ideas. No matter how much her brain screamed that he was just too big, her pussy demanded that long, wide shaft.

Powerless to resist, she spread her legs wide.

Chase needed no further invitation. Before she had time for second thoughts, his hard body was on her, his mouth capturing hers. His tongue slid between her lips, claiming and possessing her even as the thick head of his cock pressed at her entrance.

She gasped at the incredible feeling of his shaft stretching her wide. He slid slowly but unstoppably into her. She'd never imagined that she could take so much.

His rock-hard girth simultaneously caressed every part of her most sensitive inner areas. Her entire world narrowed to nothing except him as he thrust steadily, relentlessly into her.

Chase paused. Connie could feel him shaking, fighting to control himself. He filled her more than she could have dreamed possible. She balanced on the very brink of orgasm, only needing one last push to fly away.

His dark eyes were filled with raw, animal need, but he held himself still. "Connie," he said huskily.

The way he said her name held an unspoken question. In answer, she clenched around his impaling shaft.

With a heartfelt groan, Chase thrust forward a last incredible inch, finally filling her utterly. Connie was pushed over the edge, free-falling into waves of pleasure.

His strong hands seized her hips as she writhed. He withdrew and thrust, again and again, harder and harder. His breath came in great ragged gasps as he lost all control at last. He strained, burying himself deeper in her than ever, as if he was trying to make them one body, one soul.

Connie dug her fingers into his hard, muscled back... but even as she pressed against him, a tiny part of her kept a wary distance. In the middle of the storm of ecstasy, a single, simple thought remained at the center of her mind, like the calm eye of a hurricane.

I am not *going to fall for him.*

CHAPTER 6

Chase came back to himself slowly, as if spiraling down out of the sky to land. He could feel Connie's heartbeat against his chest, her pulse beating in perfect time with his own.

Our mate! In contrast to his own lassitude, his pegasus pranced in triumph, unable to keep still. *Our mate! We pleased her, we won her, she chose us! Our mate!*

Chase let out a soft, amused huff of laughter at the stallion's shameless pride in their own prowess. He pressed his face into the junction of Connie's neck and shoulder, inhaling deeply. Her flushed skin held an intoxicating trace of his own scent now. She smelled like the sky, like sex, like everything good. He could have lain there forever, breathing her in.

His stallion snorted impatiently, flicking its tail. *Up, up, swiftly! Back to the nest! Finish it, mark her, make her ours forever, ours alone. Our mate!*

"So." Connie shifted underneath him, pushing at his shoulder. "That happened."

"Mmm," Chase agreed. He reluctantly rolled onto his back to let her up. "It certainly did."

She wriggled out from under him. Chase put his arms behind his head, admiring her lush, glorious body with lazy pleasure as she started to hunt for her clothes.

"And now we've got it out of our system." Connie's voice was muffled as she pulled her top back over her head. "So we can forget this and move on."

Chase laughed. Then, abruptly, he stopped. "Wait. You're serious?"

Connie turned to face him, hands on her hips. "I told you. One-time sex, just to settle things. And now that you've gotten what you wanted, you have to go."

All his languid contentment slid away as he sat bolt upright. "Connie, no!"

"Leave, Chase!" She threw his clothes at him. "That was the deal, remember?"

He raked his hand through his sweaty hair, staring at her in utter dismay. "Yes, but—I thought—"

"You thought one taste of you would have me begging for more." Connie folded her arms over her chest, glaring at him. "Well, sorry to puncture your massive ego, but sleeping with you hasn't made me fall for you. Now leave me alone—unless you're going to break *another* promise to me?"

He'd had his mouth open to protest, but at her last words it snapped shut again. He groped for an explanation, excuses... but she was right.

Three years ago, he'd promised to be faithful to her. He'd thought it would be easy. Sure, before he'd met Connie, he'd enjoyed the billionaire playboy lifestyle, but as soon as he'd laid eyes on her he'd known that he'd never again so much as look at another woman. He'd *promised* her that.

And then, somehow, in a night that he couldn't even remember, he'd broken that promise.

If he broke another one now, she'd walk straight out of his life. Again.

No no NO! His stallion raged, hooves stamping, trying to force him to stand his ground.

For once, Chase bridled the beast, forcing it down. He could still feel it beating its wings furiously at the back of his mind as he slowly, reluctantly pulled on his clothes.

Connie held up a hand as he stumbled toward the door. "Oh, and Chase?"

He spun round so fast, he nearly lost his balance. "Yes?"

There was not the slightest hint of regret or indecision in her expression as she met his eyes. "I'll see you at the airfield tomorrow. What we... what happened doesn't change anything. We've still got a race to win."

She shut the apartment door in his face. Chase stared blindly at it. He wanted nothing more than to kick it down again, to demand that she love him as fervently and passionately as he loved her.

Because that worked so well for you last time, didn't it?

He knew he was overwhelming and impetuous and generally an all-round massive pain in the ass. Enough people had told him so, on a daily basis, pretty much his entire life.

But he'd always assumed that his fated mate would *like* that about him. Growing up, he'd just thought one day that he'd meet his mate, sweep her off her feet, and carry her off triumphantly into the sunset.

Three years ago, he'd met Connie. And she'd taken one look at him, and run away as fast as her legs could carry her.

Admittedly, in retrospect it *might* have been the wrong tactic to propose to her before even asking her name.

Chase had spent an entire month hanging round Kilkenny Airport every single day, under the excuse of taking flying lessons from her father, just for the chance to be near her. When she'd finally spoken to him again at last, her words—"Pass me that torque wrench"—were the most beautiful poetry he'd ever heard.

A month to get her to talk to him. Another month of slowly, so slowly winning her trust, persuading her that he wasn't just some flighty playboy trying to get into her pants.

She'd finally, *finally* let him take her out on a date. One date turned into two, three, more...

They'd spent a single, glorious month together as a couple. Even though she'd never let him get further than a few stolen kisses, it had been the best month of his entire life.

And then, just when she'd seemed ready to fully let him into her heart at last, he'd thrown it all away.

He still didn't know what had happened. Connie had called him to invited him round to her apartment that night 'for dinner', with a shyness that had made the subtext clear. He'd been so jubilant and nervous that the hours until the evening had seemed endless. He'd gone out to his club for a drink, just one, to pass the time.

The next thing he knew, he'd woken up in bed with two women he'd never met before, and Connie staring at him from the doorway with shocked, hurt eyes.

And then she'd turned on her heel, and walked out of his life.

Not again. Not this time.

Chase took a deep breath, straightening his shoulders. Much as he longed to charge back immediately, trying to explain things to her right now would be like running a race while wearing shackles. He was hobbled by the fact that there was so much he wasn't allowed to tell her. If only she understood that he was a shifter, and she was his mate... but that was impossible.

But that was about to change.

∼

Connie's roof turned out to have excellent cellphone reception. Chase sat cross-legged on the tiles, impatiently hitting *Redial* over and over again. Happily, it took a mere eighteen attempts before someone picked up.

"Chase," growled his cousin's irate Irish voice. "It is *one o'clock* in the *fucking morning.*"

"Killian?" Chase blinked. "That you? What are you doing with my father's phone?"

"Handling his business calls for him while he's on vacation. And it took me and your mom eight solid months of arguing with him to persuade him to take this break, so no, I am *not* putting you through. Whatever crisis you're having this time can wait."

"No, it really can't." Unable to sit still, Chase bounced to his feet, pacing back and forth along the ridgeline. "Killian, you'll never believe it. Connie's here!"

There was a moment of stunned silence from the other end of the line. "Your *mate?*"

"Yes!" Words poured out of him uncontrollably at being able to talk to someone who would understand. "And she's talking to me again, and I proposed, and her dad's in hospital, and I saved her from a fire, and—your detectives were wrong, she was in America, by the way—anyway, she's back now with her plane for the Rydon Cup air race, and there's this shark shifter called Sammy Smiles who wants to kill her because he doesn't want her to win it, but I'm going to make sure she does, so he's probably going to come after me, too."

"What?" Killian said, as if none of that had made any sense whatsoever.

"Never mind, that's not the important part," Chase said impatiently. "We had sex!"

"You did *what?*" Killian sounded utterly appalled.

"And then I messed everything up," Chase admitted.

Killian heaved a deep, heartfelt sigh. "Of course you did."

"Which is why I need to talk to my father. The only way I'm going to be able to fix this is if I can tell Connie that I'm a shifter. Once she understands about mates, she'll—"

"Chase, we went through this before, three years ago," Killian interrupted. "You can tell her once you're married. That's the way it's been for hundreds of years."

"But I can't persuade her to marry me *unless* I tell her." Chase clenched his fist. "Father's the pegasus alpha. I have to persuade him to relax the rules, just this once."

"You may be the apple of your father's eye—God knows why—but he's not going to put all of our kind at risk. Not even for you. The rules of secrecy are there for a reason, Chase. We can't risk ordinary people finding out about us. Unless you're willing to issue a formal challenge, you can't change our laws."

His stallion bared its teeth, ears flattening. *Fight the alpha. Take the herd. Win our mate!*

Chase mentally recoiled from the thought. He loved his father, and wouldn't dream of challenging him. For pegasus shifters, dominance fights were always to the death. Murdering his own father would *not* be a good start to a long-term relationship with Connie.

Plus, of course, Chase would immediately inherit the entire family business. He'd spent almost his entire life running away at top speed from *that* responsibility.

"Look," Killian said more gently, interpreting Chase's glum silence. "I know how much this means to you. Tell you what, I've got a few business things to sort out up here, but I'll come down as soon as I can and talk to her myself, okay? I think she likes me."

Chase perked up a little. Connie *had* gotten along well with Killian, on the few occasions they'd met. His older cousin was just the sort of person Connie admired—steady, reliable, serious. As the CFO of Tiernach Enterprises, he'd gained a lot of respect in both the business and shifter communities, which added to his natural air of authority. Connie would listen to him.

"Thanks, Killian," he said gratefully, sinking back down. "I owe you one. Again."

Another deep sigh. "That's me. Rescuing you from responsibility, every time." Killian paused a moment. "If you *do* win her, does that mean you'll come back? Last time you were dating her, you were full of plans to settle down. Will you finally take your place in the family business, like your father's always wanted?"

Chase shuddered, shying away from the idea like a horse from a saddle. But still... "Maybe. I like being a firefighter, I really do. But it's a dangerous job. I wouldn't want Connie to be fretting every time I went to work."

"Come to the Dark Side." Killian deepened his voice. "We have *spreadsheets.*"

"Only you could make finance sound even more boring than it

actually is." Chase kicked his feet, gazing up at the stars. "I suppose I'll have to. That's how it goes, isn't it? Find your mate, get married, become responsible…"

"Some of us skip straight to the last one," Killian murmured.

"I'm grateful to you for that," Chase said, meaning it. "You say I'm the golden boy, but you're the one who's my dad's right-hand man. I should be more like you."

"I don't recommend it," Killian said, sounding rather wistful. "I haven't found *my* mate, after all."

"When you do, I bet you won't have half the trouble I've had." Beneath him, he could feel Connie's exact location. It was physically painful to resist the way she pulled at him, a throbbing ache deep in his bones. "You've always been able to control your stallion. Not like me. I can't even sit still right now."

"I'll be down to help as soon as I can. Just don't make things worse, okay? Listen. Why don't you go out, find a club? Drink and dance and distract yourself from all this."

"No clubs," Chase said sharply. "No drinking. Not after last time."

"I'm sorry, I wasn't thinking. That was tactless." Killian paused. "But Chase, you *should* go find something to keep yourself busy. Otherwise you'll be singing under her window or setting fire to the place or some other harebrained scheme, five minutes after I hang up. I know you."

Killian *did* know him. Chase drummed his fingertips on the roof, thinking. He couldn't leave Connie unprotected, but he really would go out of his mind with restlessness if he had nothing to do except stare wistfully at the roof between them. Maybe, if he asked one of the other members of his fire crew to stand guard for him for a short time…

A slow smile spread across his face. "There *is* something I need to do. But I'm going to need some money."

"What have I done," Killian muttered under his breath. "Chase, you asked for an extra two million just six months ago. What happened to that?"

"I spent it," Chase said. "Obviously. Can I have some more?"

Killian sighed yet again. "How much do you need?"

"Tell you what." Chase's grin widened. "I'll just send you the check."

CHAPTER 7

Connie stretched as she woke, sleepily reaching out across the bed. Her questing fingers found nothing but air. The mattress next to her was empty.

A jolt of panic raced through her. She sat bolt upright, and had a confusing few seconds staring blankly at the empty space on the bed before her brain fully woke up and overruled her irrational heart.

Of course Chase isn't there. I kicked him out.

I can't believe he actually left.

She realized that part of her had been utterly convinced that he would find some way to sneak back in. At some deep level, she'd been expecting to wake up to his cocky, unrepentant grin and a torrent of nonsense explaining why he'd simply *had* to spend the night with her after all.

Connie checked under the bed. Still no Chase.

He really is honoring our deal. I slept with him, so now he'll leave me alone.

Just like I wanted.

I should feel happy about this.

Then she heard someone moving around quietly in the second room of the apartment, on the other side of the bedroom door.

Her heart skipped a beat, even as she buried her face in her hands and groaned. Of course he hadn't actually left. No doubt he was filling her tiny combined kitchen/living room with roses or iguanas or God only knew what he considered to be a romantic gesture.

Without bothering to pull on her robe, Connie marched over to the bedroom door and yanked it open. "Chase, I told you—"

It wasn't Chase.

Connie recoiled so hard she bruised her naked butt against the door handle. "Who the hell are you?"

The man turned quickly at her shout. He was tall and muscled, with short brown hair in a vaguely military cut. There was something about his dark eyes that made some deep, primal part of Connie's psyche cower back in instinctive fear. Whoever he was, this man was *dangerous*.

"Chase!" Connie grabbed the first thing that came to hand—a pillow—and flung it at the intruder. "Help!"

The man ducked the pillow, but Connie had already seized her bedside lamp. Brandishing it like a baseball bat, she charged him, swinging for his head with her full strength.

Reflexively, the man flung up one hand, seizing the body of the lamp. White fire flared. Connie yelped, dropping the lamp as the suddenly hot metal bit her skin.

"Please," the man said quickly, holding up both hands. "Do not be alarmed. I mean you no harm."

Wide-eyed, Connie stared at the scorched lamp now lying on the carpet, then back at the man. "What *are* you?"

"A friend of Chase." The man sighed, rubbing his face. "I am very sorry, but I am afraid I have no choice but to start this conversation again. Please forgive me."

Connie would have backed away from him, but she was abruptly frozen by his burning eyes. Terror-stricken, she could do nothing to resist as he reached out to touch her forehead.

Fire flared.

Connie blinked. There was a strange man in her front room.

However, he was kneeling on the ground with his eyes closed and his hands in the air. He looked more like a hostage than an intruder.

"Chase asked me to guard you while he ran an errand," the man said, very rapidly, as she drew in her breath to yell. "He was worried that Sammy Smiles might attack you in your sleep. I am Fire Commander Ash, of the East Sussex Fire and Rescue Service. May I show you my identification?"

Connie eyed him warily, casting around for a weapon. For some reason, her bedside lamp was lying in the middle of the floor. She picked it up. The metal was oddly warm in her hand as she held the lamp high, ready to bring it down on the man's head if he was lying. "Okay. But slowly."

Connie tensed as the man reached into his jacket, but true to his word he just pulled out a leather wallet. He flipped it open, silently displaying the metal shield inside.

Feeling a little silly, she lowered her impromptu weapon. "Oh. Um. Nice to meet you, Commander Ash. I'm sorry if I startled you. Chase didn't tell me you were coming."

"So I gathered," Commander Ash said, a touch grimly. "I believe I shall have words with him about that."

He was still on his knees, although he'd lowered his hands. "Uh, you can get up now, if you want," Connie offered. "I promise I won't try to brain you. Would you like some coffee?"

Ash cleared his throat, eyes still closed. "Ah. Perhaps you would care to put on some clothes first?"

Connie looked down at herself.

"Yes," she said, her voice going rather higher-pitched. "Yes, that would be a good idea."

∼

Even with clothes on, conversation with Ash proved to be an uphill struggle. The Fire Commander was perfectly polite, but so blandly noncommittal that Connie gave up on questioning him at all. He seemed content to sit in utter silence, gazing thoughtfully into the depths of the coffee she'd offered him. He exuded such an intimidating aura of reserve, Connie found herself involuntarily edging backward in her chair.

Ash abruptly looked up from his contemplation of his untouched coffee, his head turning toward the door. A moment later it slammed back on its hinges, and Chase bounced into the room.

"Oh good, you're up!" he said cheerfully to Connie. "I see you've met my Commander."

"Twice," Ash said under his breath. He looked hard at Chase.

Chase's grin slid off his face. Connie had an odd sense of some unspoken communication going on between the two men for a moment.

"Oh," Chase said in a small voice. He turned to Connie. "I'm sorry about that. Next time I'll remember to warn you."

"Next time?" Connie rolled her eyes. "Next time I throw you out of my apartment, don't take that as meaning I need you to provide someone to replace you."

Chase's grin reappeared. "Ah, so there *will* be a next time?"

"Next time is about to be right now, if you don't stop smirking at me," Connie informed him.

Commander Ash got to his feet. "I believe that my presence is no longer required."

"It was, uh, nice meeting you," Connie told him, with as much sincerity as she could muster. "Thank you for watching over me, anyway. Sorry for threatening you with a lamp."

"Please accept my sincere apologies as well," Commander Ash said, which was rather weird given that *she'd* been the one threatening *him*. With a last inscrutable look at Chase, he left.

"You tried to hit Commander Ash with a lamp?" Chase sounded utterly tickled.

Connie glared at him as she gathered up the coffee cups. "You're lucky I didn't actually take a swing at him. Honestly, Chase, what were you *thinking*?"

"I didn't mean to surprise you. I thought you'd never even know he'd been here."

Connie dumped the coffee cups into the sink with a loud clatter. "Really not helping your case, you know."

"That came out a little different to how I intended," Chase admitted. "I only meant, I planned to get back before you woke up. But I got delayed."

"Delayed doing what?" Connie said suspiciously, her back to him as she rinsed out the cups.

"Shopping," Chase said, as if this was a perfectly reasonable thing to have been doing before dawn.

"Shopping?" Connie turned around to stare at him. "What were you—"

She stopped mid-sentence. Chase was down on one knee, holding up an engagement ring with an enormous solitaire diamond.

"Constance West, will you marry me?" he said, utterly seriously.

Connie threw up her hands. "Chase, I've turned you down twice already. What on earth makes you think I've changed my mind?"

Well, apart from the absolutely incredible sex...

Connie stomped down on the traitorous thought. Fantastic sex couldn't make up for Chase's reckless, unreliable behavior. They couldn't spend *all* their time in bed.

"I didn't really ask properly before. Now I am." He held up one hand, forestalling her interruption. "Please, just hear me out. I love you, Connie. I always have, from the moment we first met, and I always will. I know you think that's crazy, but it's true. And there's a very good reason why I *know* it's true... but unfortunately, I can't tell you what that is until after we're married. So: Will you marry me?"

Connie stared at him.

"I also chartered a jet to Vegas," Chase added. "So we can get married today, I can tell you everything, and then we can still be back well in time for the race."

"You," Connie said slowly, "are *certifiably insane.*"

He didn't move. "If you don't like what I tell you, then we can get an annulment straight away. Please, Connie. Marry me, and I swear this will all make sense. Trust me."

Connie pinched the bridge of her nose, taking deep breaths until she could trust herself to speak without yelling. "No. I am not marrying you. For God's sake, Chase, we've barely even spent any time together!"

"We've known each other for three years," he argued. "Lots of people get married in less time than that."

"Three months over three years! The time when we weren't in contact doesn't count!"

"It does to me," Chase said softly. "I thought of you every day."

And I thought of you every night...

"Fantasies of some idealized versions of each other don't mean anything," she said ruthlessly. "You don't know me, Chase. No matter how much you think you do, you don't. I mean, you didn't even know that I don't like diamonds."

Chase's expression inexplicably brightened. Carelessly tossing the diamond ring aside, he rummaged in his pocket.

"Constance West," he said, pulling out a vintage gold ring set with three fabulous fire opals, "will you marry me?"

Connie's mouth hung open.

"I *did* remember that you'd mentioned once that you didn't care much for diamonds," Chase explained, offering her the ring. "But I know you also like traditions, so I thought I'd better try a very traditional ring first. Anyway, this one reminded me of that pendant you used to wear, so I thought you might like it."

"You bought *two* engagement rings," Connie said weakly. "In the middle of the night."

"Well, I found a jeweler who lived above her shop, so then it was just a case of shouting loud enough to wake her up. And then convincing her that it would be worth her while to open up." He looked a little sheepish. "I, um, actually bought five rings. I also have one with your birthstone, one with emeralds to match your eyes, and an Irish Claddagh ring."

Connie stared at him yet again.

"I have difficulty saying no to pretty things," Chase admitted.

Connie folded her arms. "Well, we both know *that's* certainly true."

Chase winced, but didn't back down. "Connie, I'm deadly serious about this. I need to marry you. Please?"

For a mad moment, Connie entertained the idea of actually going through with it, just to finally get an insight into his peculiar head. Maybe there *was* some great secret that would explain everything...

Her common sense ruthlessly crushed the silly thought. Of course there was no so-called secret, no rational reason for his erratic behavior. If he wasn't genuinely mentally ill, then he had to be just playing her, in some private, twisted joke.

"No," she repeated, hoping he hadn't noticed her hesitation. "Now get up. We have a plane to fly."

CHAPTER 8

Chase fought to contain the grin that wanted to spread across his face as he followed Connie to the airplane hanger.

She hesitated! She definitely hesitated before she said no. I'm making progress!

His stallion flicked its tail sullenly. *Slow progress. Too slow.*

It wasn't in the pegasus's nature to be patient. Or, if he was honest with himself, his own. Even though he treasured any tiny hint of Connie softening toward him, he couldn't help but want to accelerate the process.

Fortunately, he had the perfect opportunity.

Don't worry, he told his stallion, as Connie unlocked the hanger doors. *We're going to fly for her. That's sure to impress her.*

His pegasus perked up, prancing on the spot. *Yes! No one is faster, no one swifter, no one stronger than us! Show our mate! Shift, shift, now!*

Chase's lips quirked at the stallion's rampant enthusiasm. *Not that sort of flying.*

"Here she is," Connie said, rolling the big sliding door back.

Chase let out a long, low whistle of appreciation.

The vintage Spitfire gleamed like a work of art. Even parked in the hanger, the venerable WWII warplane looked ready to leap up into the air at any moment. It sat back on its wheels like a crouching beast, its single propeller pointed toward the sky, eternally keeping watch for Nazi planes.

"Hello, baby," Connie said to her plane, her voice soft.

Chase would have given anything to have her speak to *him* that way. "She's even more beautiful than I remember. New paint job?"

Connie nodded, stroking the plane's gleaming olive-green hide. "Battle of Britain squadron colors. It's not historically accurate, given that she's a Mark IX, but I flew her at a big World War II memorial event a few months back and they wanted the classic camouflage colors on her. I think it suits her, anyway."

"She's stunning." Chase noticed the way that Connie stiffened slightly as he approached the plane. He carefully kept his hands behind his back as he circled the vintage warbird. "You've kept her in absolutely perfect condition."

"And I want her to stay that way." Connie turned to face him, putting her hands on her hips. "Chase, I'm taking a huge risk here. I need to hear you say that you understand what's at stake. Do you even know how much a plane like this is worth?"

"About two and a half million dollars," Chase said absently, still admiring the plane. "Not including brokers fees."

Connie's eyebrows shot up. "How did you know that?"

"I kept an eye out for any news about Spitfires, looking for clues about where you were." Chase shrugged. "One was up for auction a little while ago. Though that one was a standard single-seater Mark IX. I suspect yours would be worth more."

"A lot more, actually." Connie pointed up at the two glass bubbles of the cockpits, one behind the other on top of the plane. "There are fewer than ten of these trainer Mark IXs still in the sky, and they're the only way a non-pilot can ever experience the thrill of flying in a Spitfire. People will pay a *lot* of money for a ride. Dad might get the occasional win from air racing, but the vast bulk of our income comes from passenger flights. This is my livelihood I'm trusting you with, Chase."

And it's your mother's plane. The one she restored from a twisted wreck, by hand, over decades. It's not just your livelihood, Connie. It's your heart.

But Chase knew that Connie would never say that out loud. She was so determinedly pragmatic, she hated to admit to being influenced by emotion.

"I know what you're trusting me with," Chase said gently. "And you can trust me. I promise."

He regretted saying it the instant the words were out of his mouth. Connie's lips compressed, as she no doubt remembered just how badly he'd kept the last promise he'd made to her, three years ago.

"I'll be in the flight instructor's cockpit," Connie said, pointing to the rear cockpit. "Both cockpits have full controls, so either one of us can fly the plane, but only I'll have the switch which toggles between the two cockpits. If I think that you're being at all reckless, I *will* throw that switch and take control back from you."

"Understood." Chase moved toward the front cockpit, ready to swing himself up.

Connie stopped him with a hand flat against his chest. "Let me make this crystal clear. If you value your balls, do not make me throw that switch."

"I won't. I hope to have a lot of future use for them, after all." He cocked a grin at her, which she did not return. "Can I get into the plane now?"

Connie hesitated, clearly searching for any other excuse to keep him out of the cockpit.

She really, really doesn't want me to do this. Maybe I should suggest she flies, and I navigate...

His pegasus pawed at the ground, snorting angry denial. *No! She must see our strength, our speed! We must fly, or we will not win our mate!*

His stallion had a point. Chase was pretty sure that no hero had ever won a fair maiden with an impressive feat of map reading.

He lightly pushed Connie's hand aside. "It's going to be pretty difficult for me to win the race for you if you won't even let me into the plane, you know."

Connie grudgingly stepped to one side. "All right. I'll take her up, and then once we're in level flight I'll hand over control to you. Don't make me regret this."

～

It was a beautiful day for flying. The old warbird soared like an eagle over the sparkling sea, its wings cleanly cutting through the air. The land was just a distant smudge behind them. Clear blue sky spread out before them, open, inviting.

The plane was a living thing, all around him, every tiny shiver and tilt transmitted directly to his awareness. He could feel it flex underneath him, leaping eagerly in response to every minuscule movement of his hands. It was like the Spitfire's body had become his own.

It was *exactly* like shifting.

The plane even had a mind of its own, just like his own stallion. This was a perfectly-honed weapon of war, with a proud history of defending Britain's skies from evil. It didn't want to cruise sedately in level flight. It wanted to swoop and dive and dogfight. It may have had the form of a machine, but it had the soul of a pegasus.

His own pegasus spread its wings, sharing the plane's exhilaration. Flying with Connie in a plane wasn't *quite* the same as carrying her in the pegasus mating ritual, but it was close enough that the stallion found it intensely arousing. Chase gritted his teeth, trying to ignore his raging erection and concentrate on the controls.

"You're doing good." Even through the tinny earpiece, the surprise in Connie's voice was obvious. "Nice and steady. How does it feel?"

"I don't think I can describe it," Chase said into his headset, wishing he'd worn looser pants. "I'm getting it under control now, though. Talk me through the race circuit, while I keep getting a feel for how she handles. Then we'll try a practice run."

"Okay," Connie said. "How much do you know about the Rydon Cup?"

"I've never seen it flown, but I've read a little about it," Chase replied, as he eased the Spitfire through a sequence of elegant banking turns. "It's a handicap race, right?"

"Right. The planes start the circuit at different times, set by the race organizers. The idea is that if everyone flew perfectly, they'd all finish together. That way it's more a test of who's the best pilot rather than just who's got the best plane."

Chase gave the Spitfire a bit more throttle, and grinned as the engine's deep snarl kicked up a notch. "And we've got the best of both. The other planes aren't going to know what hit them."

He was pretty sure Connie was glaring at the back of his head from the rear cockpit. "Don't get cocky. Our handicap is pretty substantial. The race organizers have never had a WWII warplane enter before—all the other planes are modern light aircraft. The judges spent a lot of time debating a fair starting position. They've erred on the side of caution, and put us about halfway down the line-up. You're going to have to fly extremely well to make up for the handicap."

"No problem." The Spitfire was as responsive as his own wings. "She may be a grand old lady, but she's raring to go. I bet she'll fly rings round those young upstarts."

"Just remember that we have to stay within the race corridor, otherwise we're eliminated. That's where I come in. I'll be keeping us on course. If I give you a heading, you have to respond *instantly*, understand? No arguing, no messing around, no improvisation."

"You're the boss," Chase said. "How tight are the course turns?"

"To stick to the ideal line, pretty tight. We can expect to be pulling two, maybe three Gs on the turns. There's also the notorious hairpin corner, near the end of the race."

"I've heard of that," Chase said. "Last year a couple of planes crashed trying to make that one, right?"

"Yes, it's a dangerous maneuver. Fortunately, it's been enough of a problem that the organizers have decided pilots can circle round counter-clockwise there this year, if they don't want to risk the hairpin turn. We will *definitely* be circling."

"What?" Chase protested. "Where's the fun in that?"

"The fun of not ripping the wings off a priceless antique plane," Connie retorted tartly. "The turn's technically within the Spitfire's capabilities, but I'm not risking it. I mean it, Chase. Don't even think about it."

Chase silently patted the Spitfire's instrument panel. *Don't worry, girl. I won't hold you back. We'll show her what you can do.*

"Chase," Connie said suspiciously. "You're thinking about it, aren't you?"

Chase let out a rueful laugh. "You may think that I don't know you, but you *definitely* know me."

"Unfortunately," Connie muttered. "Listen to me very carefully, Chase Tiernach. I *will* take back control of the plane from you if I think you aren't going to be sensible on the hairpin. And then I will rip off your balls and wear them as earrings."

"Earmuffs," Chase corrected cheerfully. "They're too big for earrings. You should know."

"Chase," Connie growled.

"Fine, fine. I promise, no hairpin. I'll make sure that we're well in the lead by that point, so we can do the turn the slow way. No problem." Chase took a firmer grip on the steering column. "Shall we do a practice run?"

"Okay. The actual course is half over the sea, half over the land, starting and ending at Shoreham Airport. But we'll do the whole thing over the sea for now, just in case…" Connie trailed off.

"Just in case I crash," Chase finished for her. He rolled his eyes. "Stop being so nervous, Connie. I've never crashed a plane."

"What *have* you crashed?" Connie asked suspiciously.

"Never you mind." Chase gunned the engine to drown out any further discussion on the matter. "Let's go."

Connie gave him the first heading, and Chase obediently turned the plane, pitching the nose upward as he did so.

Show me what you've got, old girl…

The Spitfire climbed like a homesick angel. Chase laughed out loud in sheer delight. Connie muttered a soft curse in his earpiece, but didn't tell him to be more cautious. She too knew that the best strategy for the race would be to gain as much height as possible at the start, so that they'd be able to dive if they needed to get a speed boost later on.

Connie called the first turn point. Chase tipped the Spitfire up on one wing, banking while still climbing. The harness straps cut into his chest as the plane whipped through the turn, as fast and deadly as a hunting falcon.

His pegasus spread its wings and soared along with the plane, filled with fierce delight. *Faster!* it urged him. *Show our speed, win our mate!*

A distant speck in the sky caught Chase's eye as he banked through the next turn under Connie's direction. He craned his neck, peering through the glass bubble of the cockpit.

"Connie," he said. "You cleared our flight path, right?"

"Of course I did. Air traffic control are keeping this area free for us. Why?"

"No reason," Chase said, his forehead creasing as he stared hard at the rapidly-approaching speck.

A rival! His pegasus bared its teeth. *Overfly him, swoop, strike!*

Hush, Chase told the aggressive stallion absently as he tried to identify the other flyer. *Of course it isn't a rival.*

Even from a distance, the bat-wing silhouette clearly wasn't a pegasus. He would have said it was a dragon, except that it was much too small. He knew all the dragon shifters living in Brighton—including his own teammate, Daifydd Drake—and all of them were at least the length of a bus.

This dragon, if dragon it was, looked to be about the size of a large horse. About the size of his own pegasus, in fact, which explained why his own stallion had mistaken it for a challenger. It was a poisonous emerald-green, which wasn't a dragon color Chase had ever seen before. There was something not quite right about its tail, too...

"Chase!" He jumped at Connie's shout. "I gave you the heading twice! Why aren't you turning?"

"Sorry." Chase hastily changed course, the plane lurching as he jerked it roughly round. "I got distracted."

"Distracted by what? It's empty sky out there."

"That's what you think," Chase muttered, too quietly to be picked up by the microphone.

The other shifter was approaching swiftly now, on an intercept course with the Spitfire. Chase couldn't imagine that it could possibly have failed to notice them. The Spitfire was loud enough that the shifter would have to be stone deaf not to have heard the plane.

Maybe it's just having some fun? It probably doesn't realize I can see it.

Chase had occasionally buzzed light aircraft himself, just for the challenge of matching speed and course with them. A normal human pilot wouldn't be able to see a mythic shifter like a dragon or a pegasus, not if it didn't want to be seen.

Deliberately, he tipped the Spitfire first to one side, then the other, waggling the wings in hello.

"What are you doing?" Connie demanded.

"Just, uh, a little crosswind," he lied, still watching the other shifter.

It hadn't responded to his impromptu greeting. Chase tried to mind-speak it, but it was like shouting at a closed door. The other shifter was deliberately blocking all psychic communication.

I'm starting to get a bad feeling about this.

It was close enough now that he could see that it *was* roughly dragon-shaped, with a long neck and wedge-shaped reptilian head. But it only had two legs, not four. Its curved, muscular tail ended in a scorpion's barb, the needle-sharp point at least two feet long.

Bloody hell, it's a wyvern!

Chase had never seen one before. He'd never *heard* of someone who'd actually seen one before. They were so rare, they bordered on legendary, even amongst mythic shifters. They were bogeymen in the stories shifter kids told around campfires: *Stone heart, poison blood, acid breath...*

The wyvern opened its jaws, and spat out a fine, dense cloud of mist.

Chase slammed the plane into a near-vertical climb. The plane shrieked in protest, threatening to stall, but Chase forced it upward. The cloud of acid missed them by inches.

"What are you *doing*?" Connie screamed in his ear as the plane hurtled straight up toward the sun.

"Sudden emergency!" Chase desperately craned his neck, trying to see where the wyvern had gone. "No time to explain!"

He caught sight of the wyvern, only a dozen feet off their tail. Its wings cut through the air like knives. Even with the Spitfire's engine roaring at full throttle, it was catching up with them.

Let's see how you handle this...

Chase flipped the Spitfire nose-over-tail, tumbling into an upside-down dive. The wyvern futilely snatched at them as they shot underneath it with inches to spare, its wicked claws snapping shut on empty air.

"Chase!" Connie's furious voice blasted through the headset. "I'm giving you three seconds to straighten out or I swear to God I am taking back control of this plane!"

"If you hit that switch, we'll both be dead!" Chase yelled back.

He pulled the Spitfire out of the dive, praying that they'd gained enough distance from the wyvern to be able to risk a straight dash back toward land. At the moment, they were too far from Brighton for Chase to be able to psychically contact the rest of his fire team. Commander Ash in his Phoenix form could drive away the wyvern, if Chase could just get close enough to the city to reach him...

DANGER!

Chase instinctively jerked the steering column in response to his stallion's shriek, spinning the Spitfire on its axis. He was almost too late. The wyvern's acid cloud of breath clipped one wingtip, eating dozens of small holes into its metal skin.

"Chase!" Connie must have seen the acrid vapor steaming off the acid-etched metal, but of course she had no idea the real source of the damage. "That's it, I'm taking back control. Three!"

"Connie, no!" Chase shouted frantically. "Please! *Trust me!*"

The wyvern's sleek light, sleek body and disproportionally large wings made it lethally fast, much faster than any dragon he'd ever seen. It took all of Chase's flying skill just to stay ahead of it. It matched him turn for turn, no matter what evasive maneuvers he tried.

"Two!" Connie continued relentlessly, as the sea and sky spun madly around them.

She was going to do it. She was going to take back control. And the instant she leveled out the plane, the wyvern would catch them.

"One!"

There was only one thing Chase could do.

He hit the eject button.

CHAPTER 9

"I have control," Connie said, flipping the override switch. "Chase, you are so—"

In front of her, Chase's cockpit abruptly blew open. Chase stood up on his seat, the wind whipping his hair and flight suit. She distinctly saw him drop his unopened parachute back into the cockpit.

Then he launched himself out of the plane.

"What the actual *fuck*?" Connie breathed in disbelief.

Instinctively, she wheeled the Spitfire over on one wingtip, trying to follow his falling figure. She caught the barest glimpse of him as he plummeted toward the distant waves—and then the Spitfire lurched sickeningly.

To Connie's horror, the strange corrosion she seen earlier was spreading further, Swiss-cheese holes appearing in the surface of the Spitfire's left wing. It was as if invisible acid was eating away at the metal. With a *clunk*, the left flap pinwheeled away, the control lever going dead in her hand.

The plane yawed, tipping to the left. Connie fought to steady it, desperately trying to keep the plane level with only half the controls operational.

Out of nowhere, rain pattered across the cockpit. Instantly, pits appeared in the glass, obstructing her view. Through the warped cockpit, she saw more holes appearing in the nose of the plane, eating into the engine housing.

The Spitfire's engine coughed, twice, and died.

"*No!*" Connie shouted, as if she could keep the plane in the air through sheer willpower.

She knew this plane inside and out. She'd worked on every part of it with her own two hands. Now she used that encyclopedic knowledge, drawing on every trick she knew as the Spitfire fell like a dying star.

Screaming defiance, Connie leveled out the wings, stopping the plane's sickening spin. But it was still falling like a stone, nose-first, straight down. If the plane hit the sea like that, it would be like slamming into solid rock. The Spitfire would explode into a million pieces.

Connie inched the plane's nose up, fighting gravity tooth and nail. Agonizingly slowly, the plane responded, straightening up.

If I can just straighten it out... skim across the water like a skipping stone...

Even as she wrestled with the controls, she knew it was futile. Even hitting the water belly-first rather than nose-first, the plane would still sink—in one piece, perhaps, but it was still doomed.

The only sensible thing to do was to hit the eject button. To abandon the plane, and save herself.

NO!

The hungry sea rushed up, eager to swallow both her and the Spitfire in one mouthful. Closing her eyes, Connie prepared to die with her plane.

Glass shards cascaded over her as the cockpit exploded. Connie had only the briefest impression of something huge and black lunging at her, before it grabbed her by the collar of her flight suit. With a powerful tug, it yanked her straight out of the cockpit.

Connie's feet swinging sickeningly over empty air. The... *thing* had her by the scruff of the neck. Her flight suit cut into her armpits, constraining her as she tried futilely to see what had grabbed her. She dangled as helpless as a kitten carried by its mother.

Then it dropped her.

Screaming, Connie flailed helplessly as she plummeted toward the sea. She only fell for a moment, though, before landing solidly on a broad, warm back. Sobbing in terror, Connie clutched at the horse's gleaming black neck.

Wait a second.

...A horse?

Connie raised her face, unable to believe the evidence of her senses. Yet she was, undeniably, sitting on a horse. A *winged* horse. It had magnificent, iridescent blue-black feathers, like an enormous raven. Its long mane whipped at her face as it flew steadily onwards.

I've died, Connie thought blankly. *I've crashed and burned and now I'm dead. And a big winged horse is carrying me up to Heaven.*

"Are you an angel?" she asked the horse, her voice quavering uncontrollably.

The horse curved its neck, one intelligent black eye looking back at her. It let out an unmistakably amused snort.

And suddenly, impossibly, Connie knew exactly what it was. Or rather, *who* it was.

"Chase?"

The horse nickered, tossing its head in a nod.

It was too much. The inexplicable disaster, the crash, Chase turning into a winged horse... her overloaded brain simply gave up, refusing to try to make sense of any of it.

Connie put her cheek against Chase's warm, black neck, closed her eyes, and let him carry her away from it all.

∽

If Connie had been capable of being surprised anymore, she would have been startled by how fast Chase's broad wings carried them back to Brighton. It took less time to get back than it had taken to fly out in the Spitfire. Soon they were once again soaring over the beach and promenade—but this time, no one squinted upward at them, pointing and waving. Pedestrians carried on about their business without even an upward glance as the winged horse's shadow swept over them.

Connie was beyond wondering about everyone's curious incuriosity to the impossibility soaring over their heads. Her mind and body had both gone numb. Only one thought repeated in her head, over and over, inescapably.

I lost my mother's plane.

I lost my mother's plane.

Chase descended in a tight spiral, centered on a tall, elegant apartment block. The building's large, flat roof was beautifully planted with lush rosebushes around a vibrant green lawn. Chase landed so gently, Connie barely felt his hooves touch down on the grass.

The pegasus went down on one knee, stretching out one wing like a ramp. When she didn't move, he bent his neck to look back at her again, the dark eye warm and concerned. He nickered, very softly. His velvet-soft nose nudged her limp foot.

Connie slid gracelessly off his back. Her knees couldn't support her. She would have collapsed in a heap, but suddenly Chase's strong arms were around her.

"It's okay, Connie," he said softly. "I've got you. It's going to be okay."

"It is *not*." Abruptly, irrationally furious, Connie shoved futilely at his hard chest. "It's not okay, Chase! Nothing is ever going to be okay, ever again! I crashed, and I lost my plane, and, and, and you're a fucking horse!"

"Pegasus," Chase corrected.

"Do not *dare* argue zoology with me! Or, or mythology, or whatever fucking field of study is fucking relevant here!" Connie pounded her fist against his shoulder. He didn't flinch. "You should have told me, Chase! I crashed and, and all this time you're some sort of shapeshifter, and you should have told me!"

"I know," Chase said quietly. He kept holding her, no matter how she scratched at him. "I'm sorry."

"You should have told me," she snarled at him. Hot tears burned her eyes. "You lied. You're a fucking liar and I hate you and I never want to see you again."

Then she collapsed against Chase's chest, burying her face in his flight suit as she cried.

He let her sob, just gently cradling her as her tears soaked his chest. She could feel the rapid beat of his heart, strong and reassuring.

When she'd cried herself out, he put a finger under her chin, tipping her face up. His steady black eyes met hers.

"It's not lost, Connie," he said, with utter certainty. "We are going to get your plane back. Trust me."

Connie shook her head. "It's gone. I lost my mother's plane, Chase. The only thing I had left of her, and I destroyed it."

"You *saved* it." Chase took hold of her shoulders, making her face him square on. "I saw it sinking as I carried you away. It went down in one piece. We *will* get it back."

"How?" Connie's mind shied away from estimating the cost of any recovery mission. "It's at the bottom of the sea. It'll be impossible to recover."

One corner of Chase's mouth quirked. "Connie, you just saw me turn into a pegasus. Are you seriously going to argue with me about what's possible?"

She had to admit, he had a point.

She sniffed, swiping the back of her hand across her dripping nose. "Why didn't you tell me? About the pegasus thing, I mean."

Chase let out his breath in a long sigh. "I wasn't allowed to. The rule in my family is that we're only allowed to reveal what we truly are to our mate after marriage."

"So *that's* why you kept proposing. There really was a secret you weren't allowed to tell me." Connie paused, blinking. "Wait. Your family? Are you all... whatever you are?"

"Shifters. We're called shifters. And no, not my whole family. My mom's side of the family are all ordinary humans. But me, my cousin Killian, and my dad are all pegasi. My uncle was too, but he died when I was little."

"So there's three of you." Connie's mind reeled at the thought of there being other people who could do what Chase did. "Three shifters."

"Um. You should probably be sitting down for this bit." Gently, Chase sank down on the grass, drawing her down with him. "There are a lot more shifters than that. There's a whole hidden society of us."

Connie stared at him. "A whole *society* of people who turn into pegasus...es?"

"Pegasi. And no, of course not." Just as Connie started to relax, he added, "The vast majority of shifters are just ordinary animals—bears, wolves, lions, that sort of thing. Pegasi are very rare. Even rarer than dragons."

"Dragons," Connie echoed faintly.

"Ah, well, yes." Chase raked a hand through his hair, frowning. "I should probably tell you about those sooner rather than later, seeing as how one was responsible for crashing your plane. Well, I think technically it was a wyvern, but you said you didn't want to get into comparative mythical zoology, so let's just call it a dragon for now. Particularly since *I* can hardly believe it was really a wyvern. I thought they were just a story. Like leprechauns or unicorns."

"Oh, good," Connie said, unable to control the hysterical edge to her voice. "Everything is back to normal. You've gone back to talking a mile a minute without making the slightest bit of sense."

"I'm still trying to make sense of it myself." Chase fell silent for a moment, his eyebrows drawing together in thought. "Connie, do your hands feel cold?"

Connie blinked at the apparent non sequitur, then realized that she was shivering. "All of me feels cold."

Chase swore under his breath. "I'm an idiot. You're going into shock. Hold on a second, I need to talk to someone."

She expected him to pull out his phone, but instead he just stared off into the distance, his eyes going unfocused. After a moment, he nodded.

"Right," he said. Before she knew what was happening, he'd scooped her up, without any apparent effort. "Hugh— he's our paramedic—says you need to lie down and warm up. Let's get you inside."

There were so many questions to ask—how he could have a conversation with someone who wasn't even there, how she could have failed to see a dragon attacking her plane, where the hypothetical dragon could have come from in the first place—but abruptly, she was just too tired. She leaned her head against Chase's shoulder, closing her eyes.

"Here we are," she heard him say, and then she was sinking into a deep, soft bed. She didn't resist as he pulled off her shoes and draped a thick down comforter over her. "Feeling any better?"

"Still cold," Connie managed to get out, through her chattering teeth.

The bed dipped as he slid under the cover next to her. He curled around her, fitting his long, lean body against the curves of her back. Pressed against his warm torso, Connie's shivers finally started to ease. She burrowed her head under the covers, like a little kid hiding from monsters in the dark. Just for a moment, all she wanted to do was pretend that none of it had ever happened.

As her own shivers subsided, Connie became aware that *Chase* was shaking, ever so slightly.

"Hey," she said. "Are *you* okay?"

"I thought I'd lost you. I was fighting off the wyvern, and then I saw the plane going down, and I didn't think I was going to get to you in time…" He tightened his grip on her, burying his face in her hair. "Oh God, Connie, I nearly lost you."

She rolled over in his arms, their faces only inches away from each other. She could tell he was trying to control his expression, but his black eyes were raw and vulnerable. For all his strength and uncanny powers, it was clear that the mere thought of losing her struck him to the heart.

"But you didn't lose me." Connie put her hand on the side of his face, feeling how warm he was, how *alive*. "I'm here. We're both here."

Overcome by a sudden, powerful need, she leaned in and kissed him. He crushed her against his strong body, his mouth devouring hers desperately, as if he couldn't bear to ever let her go again.

She had a deep, instinctive desire to reaffirm life in the most basic of ways after her brush with death. Connie fumbled with the zip of his flight suit, jerking it open. The heat of his skin was the only thing that could drive away the ice in her soul.

She slid her palm down his muscled abs, and under the waistband of his boxers. He was hard already, so thick she could barely get her hand around him. Her pussy throbbed, desperate to be filled, as she worked him fast and urgently.

He knew exactly what she wanted. His powerful hands ripped her own flight suit off, the tough material tearing as easily as damp tissue paper. He gathered her breasts in his hands, pinching and teasing her erect nipples through the lace cups of her bra with delicious roughness. His mouth was hard on hers, demanding, taking.

She squeezed her fist around his cock, feeling the contrast of the velvet-soft skin over the iron-hard shaft. He growled low in his throat, his hips jerking involuntarily. Breaking off from the kiss for a moment, he grabbed her buttocks, lifting her up and spreading her wide.

He didn't even bother to tear off her panties. The wide head of his cock shoved the thin silk to one side, pushing deep into her wet folds with a single powerful thrust. His thick shaft impaled her to her core, stretching her with a pleasure so intense it was almost painful.

Unlike last time, he gave her no time to adjust to his overwhelming size. He thrust savagely, uncontrollably into her. Connie arched her back, clenching around his demanding cock with equal passion, overwhelmed by sensation. It was exactly what she needed, to lose herself utterly, even if only for a moment.

"Never again," Chase snarled, his fingers digging into her hips almost hard enough to bruise. "Never losing you. Never. Mine. Mine!"

Yes! Connie's soul sang back, echoing his fierce possessiveness. Every fiber of her being yearned to tell him *yes, yes!*

She was his, and he was hers, and nothing would ever separate them.

Yes.

Yet there was still a bit of her that held back. After a lifetime of having to be the cautious one, there was always a cold-eyed part of her mind that dispassionately evaluated every situation.

That sensible inner voice whispered that it didn't matter how urgent his body was on hers now, how fervently he gasped promises. In a day or two, someone else would catch his eye. It would be someone else's ear he whispered into, someone else's body he strained against.

When Chase gasped "Mine!" she knew he meant it... for now.

But if she replied *yes*, she would mean it forever.

Connie bit down hard on Chase's shoulder, stifling the words that wanted to rise in her throat, even as ecstasy swept her away.

CHAPTER 10

"So," Chase said softly into Connie's ear, some time later. "Constance West, will you marry me?"

Connie raised her head from his shoulder to give him a quizzical look. "I already know you're a shifter. I thought you only needed me to marry you so that you'd be allowed to tell me the truth."

"That was one reason." Chase traced the soft curves of her bare arm, wanting to memorize every inch of her beautiful body. "But mostly, I just really, really want to marry you. So? Will you?"

Connie blew out an exasperated breath. Without answering, she rolled out of the bed, searching the floor for her discarded clothes.

From a flat-out refusal, to a hesitation before refusing, to no answer. Definite progress!

Connie scowled at him. "What are you grinning about?"

Chase attempted to school his face into an appropriately somber expression, without much success. "Nothing. Just admiring the view."

Connie shot him a glare, then held up her ripped flight suit. "This is completely ruined. What am I going to wear?"

Chase slid out of bed himself. "You can borrow something of mine. This way."

"Chase, you're about a foot taller than me, not to mention a completely different shape," Connie said dubiously as he led her into his walk-in closet. "I really don't think that you're going to have anything that will fit me."

"Um." Chase slid hangers of shirts and suits aside, revealing the very back corner of the closet. "Actually, I do."

Connie blinked for a moment at the row of women's clothes. Every one was immaculate and unworn, and every one was exactly her size.

Then she groaned, rolling her eyes. "Of course you have a closet full of dresses. Heaven forbid one of your many one-night stands should have to do the Walk of Shame in last night's outfit."

"No, of course not!" Chase said indignantly. "I bought them for you. Or, well, because they reminded me of you. Sometimes I'd see something, and think *Connie would like that*, or *That could have been made for Connie*. And then I'd have to buy it. Because it was a way of showing myself that I hadn't given up hope. That one day I'd find you again, and give you these clothes, and see you in them."

"I don't know whether that's incredibly sweet or incredibly creepy." Connie sighed, and started to flick through hangers. "But I can't deny that it's convenient. I notice, by the way, that you mainly appear to have been reminded of me by lingerie."

"What can I say?" Chase grinned unrepentantly at her. "I'm an optimist."

"Chase, people who buy lottery tickets are optimists," Connie retorted as she selected a leaf-green, silk summer dress that perfectly matched the shade of her eyes. "People who go around acting as if they've already won the lottery are delusional."

Chase started getting dressed himself. "What about people who've won the lottery, but then drop the ticket, so they end up walking around backward peering at the ground, and everyone thinks they're crazy, but actually they're just taking entirely logical steps to try to recover what they lost?"

"Trust you to run away with a metaphor," Connie muttered from the depths of the dress. "You know, your big secret doesn't actually explain very much. Just because you turn into a big winged horse sometimes doesn't explain why you're so... *you*."

Chase paused in doing up his jeans.

Then he smacked himself on the forehead. "I'm a complete idiot. I forgot to tell you the most important part. The bit that explains everything."

Connie turned to face him, putting her hands on her hips. "Now this, I've got to hear."

Chase briefly wondered whether to suggest that they went up to his rooftop rose garden, for a more romantic setting. His closet had not been the backdrop he'd pictured for the most important conversation of his life.

He settled for going down on one knee instead. "Connie—"

Connie hid both her hands behind her back. "If you propose again, I swear to God I will hit you."

"This isn't another proposal. This is the reason for all the proposals. The reason I've been mad about you ever since I first saw you." Chase took a deep breath, looking earnestly up at her wary face. "All shifters have a mate. Just one single person, in all the world, who's their perfect partner. You're *my* mate, Connie. I knew it the instant we first met. And from that moment on, I've only had eyes for you. You're the only one for me, and you always will be."

Connie looked down at him, her expression completely unreadable, for a long, long moment that seemed to stretch into eternity.

Then, "Do you think I'm a *complete* idiot?" Turning on her heel, she stormed out of the closet.

"Wait!" Chase scrambled to his feet.

That didn't go quite the way I thought it would.

He caught up with her halfway across his bedroom, seizing her arm to stop her in her tracks. "I know it might sound unbelievable to you, but—"

"It *might* sound unbelievable?" Connie whirled on him, her cheeks flushed red and her eyes glittering with barely-restrained tears. "Of course it sounds unbelievable! There's some mystic force which bound you to me the instant you saw me, huh? I'm the one person in all the world for you, am I? Well, that *completely* explains everything. Except for the fact that *you cheated on me!*"

"As I keep trying to explain to you, I *didn't!*" Chase held onto her wrist. She wasn't getting away from him this time. "Connie, I swear, I did not cheat on you. I know what it looked like, but I would *never* cheat on you."

"Liar," Connie snarled.

"I'm telling the truth! I don't remember anything from that night, apart from going to the club and having one drink. I don't know what happened after that."

"Oh, come on. We both know what happened," Connie snapped. "You got blind, stinking drunk, and couldn't resist a pair of pretty girls. You've always been a playboy, and you always will be. I was stupid to think that you'd ever change."

"I'm telling you, you're my mate! It's physically impossible for me to have cheated on you!"

Chase had spent years trying to work out what had actually happened that night, but had drawn a complete blank. The women had sworn that he'd picked them up and had sex with them, but he knew, *knew* that they had to have been lying. There was no way he could have done that, no matter how drunk he'd been.

He fumbled for excuses, knowing that they sounded weak even as he said them. "Maybe they were trying to blackmail me, or, or it was some sort of prank, or—Killian!"

"Your cousin?" Connie blinked. "Are you seriously trying to blame everything on your *cousin?*"

"No, of course not. I mean, he's here!" Chase pulled her toward the door that led to the rooftop garden, his heart rising again. "He said he'd come visit, but I didn't think it would be this soon. This is great!"

If anyone could help fix the mess he'd made, it was his cousin.

∼

Chase took the stairs two at a time, hauling Connie in his wake despite her spluttered protests. His pegasus's special ability to sense people told him that Killian was spiraling in toward the landing area. Chase burst out onto the rooftop garden just in time to see his cousin's hooves settling onto the grass.

"Killian!" Chase waved frantically with his free arm. "Excellent timing! Tell Connie I'm not lying about being fated mates!"

Connie stared at him as if he'd gone mad. So did Killian.

"Chase," Connie said, not even glancing at the enormous winged horse occupying a large part of the lawn. "There's no one here."

Of course, she can't see him.

Killian was still in pegasus form, his stormcloud-gray wings half-open as if he was wondering whether to take off again. **I'm sorry,** he psychically sent to Chase. **Have I arrived at a bad time?**

"No, this is perfect," Chase replied out loud, so as not to exclude Connie from the conversation. "Go ahead and shift. It's okay, Connie knows everything now. I had to shift to save her life. That's allowed by the law, right?"

Killian let out a snort that morphed into a deep groan as he shifted back into human form. "Trust you to find a loophole."

Connie yelped, jumping backward as—from her perspective—Killian materialized out of thin air.

"Connie." Killian held out his hand to her, flashing a quick smile. "It's nice to see you again. I am very sorry to have to interrupt you on what I understand has been a very traumatic day, but I needed to check that my fool cousin was all right after the crash."

Chase cocked his head to one side. "How did you know about that so fast?"

"You know I always keep a close eye on you. It's why you're still flying around despite years of flinging yourself enthusiastically into every disaster you can find." Despite his dry words, Killian's gray eyes were concerned as he looked Chase up and down. "*Are* you in one piece? Not many shifters go wingtip-to-wingtip with a wyvern and live to tell the tale."

Connie, who had been looking back and forth between them like a spectator at a very mysterious tennis game, flinched at his words. "So it really was a wyvern that attacked my plane?"

Killian nodded gravely. "I haven't had much time to look into the matter, but in the past I've heard rumors that there's a wyvern shifter who works for criminal organizations. From what I know of your situation, I strongly suspect Sammy Smiles was behind the attack."

"How would Sammy Smiles know a wyvern?" Connie asked, sounding lost.

"I didn't have time to tell you before, but Sammy Smiles is a shifter too," Chase told Connie. He hated to drop all this on her at once, but he knew she was tough. "He's a shark. The Parliament of Shifters—that's a sort of government for our kind—has a tough time controlling sea-based shifters. Sammy's got a whole criminal gang made up of sharks and the like."

"Oh," Connie said. He could practically see her mind racing as she digested this new information. "My plane... it's in the sea. If he can turn into a shark, that means he'll be able to find it, right?"

"Yes, but we're going to get there first," Chase said confidently. "I contacted a friend while I was carrying you back to land. He's already on his way to your plane, and he'll keep it safe. No shark will get past him."

Killian shot him a curious look, but didn't ask for details. "I haven't been able to locate Sammy Smiles yet, I'm afraid. I've never met him, nor met anyone who has, so my pegasus can't track him."

"Mine can." Chase bared his teeth in a feral smile. "And I'm going to pay him a little visit."

Killian sighed. "I was afraid you were going to say that. I suppose there's absolutely nothing I can say to dissuade you."

"Nothing whatsoever," Chase agreed cheerfully.

Killian sighed again. "Then I'll stand guard over your mate while you do so. I'm assuming even you aren't daft enough to take her with you on a trip down a shark's gullet."

"I'm *not* his mate," Connie said sharply.

"Ah." Killian's eyes flicked from her to Chase and back again. "Connie, my idiot cousin has a remarkable ability to stuff all four hooves down his own throat when he's trying to explain himself. Perhaps I could be of assistance? I would be happy to answer any questions you have about shifters in general. Or, indeed, Chase in particular."

You are only going to tell her good things about me, right? Chase sent anxiously to him.

Do you want the conversation to last more than thirty seconds? Killian sent back acerbically.

Connie considered Killian, her expression warming a little. "Yes. Thank you, I would like that."

Killian turned back to Chase. "Connie and I will be fine here. I'll sense if the wyvern approaches again, and get her to safety. Are you ready to go see Sammy now?"

"Not yet." Chase clapped his hands together decisively. "First, we all have to go to the pub."

CHAPTER 11

Connie stared up at the full moon painted on the dusty sign outside the old, whitewashed building. "When he said we were going to the pub," she muttered to Killian, "I thought he was joking."

"So did I." Chase's cousin let out a long-suffering sigh as he held the oak door open for her. "I really should know better by now."

They followed Chase into the pub. Connie was startled by how cozy and clean it was inside, a stark contrast to the grimy, forbidding exterior. Even though it was only early evening, the pub was well-populated by a mixed crowd, lounging at the polished bar or relaxing in mismatched antique chairs.

A general cry of "Chase!" went up as soon as he showed his face. Chase dispensed cheery waves and a few words of greeting as they cut through the crowd.

"I take it you're a regular," Connie said to him.

Privately, she was a little surprised. She would have thought Chase would favor the sort of sleazy gambling dens that her father liked to frequent. But this pub was clearly intended for socializing, rather than hardcore drinking and shady deals.

"The Full Moon is the local shifter hangout," Chase said. "At least, it's the respectable shifter hangout. Rose makes sure everyone behaves themselves. Right, Rose?"

"That's right," the curvy, kind-eyed woman behind the bar agreed amiably.

Personally, Connie had never seen anyone less intimidating in her life. But for all she knew, Rose could turn into a bear or a tiger or who-knew-what. She still could barely believe that there was an entire society of shifters that she'd never even suspected existed.

"Connie, Killian, this is Rose Swanmay," Chase introduced them. "She runs this place. Rose, this is my cousin Killian, down from London. And this is Connie. You don't need me to tell you who *she* is."

Rose smiled at Killian, then did a double-take at Connie. "Your mate!"

Chase shot Connie a *See? I told you so* sort of smirk. She rolled her eyes at him.

"It's lovely to meet you, Connie." Rose looked thoughtful for a moment. "Just to check... you do know he's a shifter, don't you?"

"Yes," Connie replied. "And just to clarify, I am *not* his mate."

"Well, actually, I'm afraid you are," Rose said, her soft lips quirking. "Congratulations, and condolences. I'll always have a free drink and a sympathetic ear ready for you."

"Hey!" Chase protested. "I'm not that bad."

"Yes, you are," Killian muttered.

"The boys are upstairs waiting for you," Rose said to Chase. "Not that you need me to tell you that. Shall I get you the usual?"

Chase shook his head. "I'm just dropping by. Thanks, Rose."

"Why *are* we here, Chase?" Killian asked, as they followed Chase to the back of the pub.

"Because I need to meet with some people," he replied, leading them up a narrow flight of stairs. "And I wanted you to meet them, too."

Chase opened a door, revealing a small private room. Four people were seated around a small circular table. Connie recognized Commander Ash, but she didn't know the other three.

"Connie, Killian, this is my fire crew," Chase said, beaming. Then he frowned. "Or at least, some of my fire crew. Commander, where's Griff?"

"I am afraid he is indisposed," said Commander Ash, rising to his feet. "The usual problem. He sends his apologies. Ms. West, I am pleased to meet you again in, ah, better circumstances."

"Likewise," Connie muttered, unable to help blushing as she remembered their first meeting.

At least I'm wearing clothes this time.

At Ash's gesture, she seated herself gingerly on a free chair. Besides Ash, there were two other men and one woman present. Connie lifted her chin, forcing down a wave of self-consciousness as she met their stares.

Commander Ash was as coolly unreadable as the last time Connie had met him, but a muscular, red-headed man was openly curious. The curvy black woman snuggled under the red-head's arm caught Connie's eye and gave her a conspiratorial wink. In contrast, a young, handsome man with bleached white hair and pale blue eyes was scowling at Connie as if she'd personally offended him somehow.

"Griff's sick again?" Chase frowned as he plopped down onto a chair next to her. "Damn. I could really use his talent. Hugh, can't you do anything to help him?"

"If I could, don't you think I would have already?" the white-haired man snapped. He rubbed his forehead as if he had a migraine. "I can't heal everything."

Commander Ash raised one hand. "Before we go any further, there is something I must clarify first. Ms. West, are you aware that Chase is a shifter?"

"Yes, of course," Connie replied, frowning. "Why do people keep asking me that?"

"Truly, it is a mystery." Chase looked across at the red-haired man, clearly struggling to keep a straight face. "Any ideas, Dai?"

Dai's ears turned nearly as red as his hair. He appeared to find something intensely interesting about the ceiling.

The woman next to him laughed. "It's one of those annoying in-jokes," she explained to Connie. Her accent marked her as a fellow

American, making Connie feel a little less out of place. "When *I* met the crew, there were... a few misunderstandings." She held out her hand. "Virginia Drake. I'm Dai's mate."

"See!" Chase exclaimed triumphantly, as Connie shook Virginia's hand. "Independent evidence, right before your eyes! Mates *do* exist!"

"And apparently Chase is managing to make even more of a mess of things than I did," Dai murmured. He had a pleasant, deep voice with a lilting Welsh accent. "I'm not sure whether to be comforted or alarmed."

"Personally, I'm past alarmed, and well into terrified," Killian said dryly.

Ash leaned forward a little, the slight movement instantly silencing the banter. "Secondly. Are you aware that we are all—Virginia excepted—shifters as well?"

Connie shook her head, but she wasn't actually surprised. Even though the three men didn't look anything like each other—Dai huge and muscular, Hugh lean and elegant, Ash contained and controlled—there was something similar about them. On some deep, instinctive level, she could sense the power that they possessed.

She cast a sideways look at Chase, realizing that he too had that indefinable feral aura. Killian did as well, though to a lesser extent.

"Let me introduce you both to everyone." Chase waved a hand at Ash. "For those who haven't met him yet, I present Fire Commander Ash. He's the Phoenix, and yes, that's 'the', not 'a'. There's only ever one. "

Killian looked at Ash with awe, and a touch of wariness. "It's an honor, sir."

"He's kind of a big deal in the shifter community," Chase informed Connie, as though this wasn't obvious. "Oh, also, he can burn anything, and I mean *anything*. A slightly odd trait for a firefighter, if you ask me, but it's surprisingly handy."

Moving on, Chase pointed in the direction of the handsome white-haired man in the corner. "Hugh here is our paramedic, and a puzzle wrapped in a mystery wrapped in an enigma wrapped in an incredibly cranky attitude. Please question him repeatedly and persistently about what sort of shifter he is, because he says if *I* ask him one more time, he'll never heal me again."

Hugh leaned away from Chase's finger, his pained scowl deepening. "I am really looking forward to the next time you crash and break a bone."

Chase ignored this. He waved his hand at the huge red-headed man. "And this is Daifydd Drake, but everyone calls him Dai because Welsh names are ridiculous, and I say that even as an Irishman. He's a red dragon—don't worry, he's a nice dragon, not like the one who attacked your plane, Connie. He's fireproof, which is a very useful thing for a firefighter to be, obviously. And next to him is Virginia, his lovely mate who isn't a firefighter or a shifter but who *is* extremely perceptive and clever and who incidentally I hope is only going to tell you good things about me."

There was a moment of silence.

"And if you were able to follow all of *that*," Dai said ruefully to Connie, "then you really must be his mate."

Frighteningly, Connie had. Navigating through a conversation with Chase was like flying through a storm—there was no point trying to impose your own course. You just had to ride it out and see where you ended up.

"Everyone, this is my cousin Killian, who is a pegasus and Chief Financial Officer of Tiernach Enterprises," Chase said, jerking his thumb casually at Killian. "Don't ask him about his job unless you're suffering from insomnia. Really, don't."

Killian lifted a hand in a brief, embarrassed wave. "Please let me reassure you all that I am nothing like my cousin."

"And, saving the best for last, this is Connie West." Chase made a sweeping gesture at Connie like a sculptor unveiling his masterpiece. "She is the most amazing and beautiful and brave woman in the entire world, and I'm going to marry her just as soon as she stops yelling at me whenever I propose."

Connie jabbed him sharply in the arm with her elbow.

"Ow," Chase said, cheerfully. "As you can see, I've got some way to go with that. Which is why I need all of your help. Oh, and also with the wyvern and the race and all, of course."

"So I take it Chase has already told you about what happened with my plane?" Connie said, looking round at the group.

Commander Ash inclined his head. "Yes. Mythic shifters—those, like ourselves, who turn into creatures out of legend rather than ordinary animals—are able to communicate telepathically with each other. Chase has already briefed us on your situation. If there is anything we can do to assist, we are at your service."

"Thank you. I appreciate that, truly." She shot Chase a sidelong look. "Though I'm not sure how you *can* help. I don't know what Chase is thinking."

"Who ever does?" murmured Killian. "Do you actually have a plan, Chase, or are you making it up as you go along as usual?"

"I have a plan," Chase said indignantly. He hesitated. "Or... I did. Without Griff, I'm going to have to improvise a bit."

Hugh rolled his eyes. "Oh, joy."

"Who's this Griff?" Connie asked.

"Another member of our team," Chase said. "Or, well, technically he *was* a member. He's a dispatcher now, since he had to retire from firefighting. I wanted him to come with me to talk to Sammy Smiles. He can tell if people are lying, you see."

"So he's a shifter too?" Connie said.

All four firefighters exchanged glances. "Yes and no," Ash said. "But that's for Griff to explain, if he wishes."

"Chase, were you going to introduce her to John, too?" asked Dai. "Is he on his way?"

"No, he's tied up at the moment." Chase turned to Connie. "John's the friend that I mentioned earlier, the one who I asked to watch over your Spitfire. He'll stand guard over it until we can get it out of the water. He's a sea dragon shifter, so he can stay underwater indefinitely."

Commander Ash cleared his throat. "Unfortunately, that is not precisely true. John has duties on dry land, as do the rest of the crew. Ms. West, while we can help you in our free time, I am afraid that I cannot allow your predicament to compromise the safety of this city. Our responsibilities must come first."

"But I need John to help with the plane," Chase objected. "And that wyvern is still on the loose. I'll need Dai tomorrow to guard the race."

Ash shook his head. "Alpha Fire Team is scheduled to be on duty tomorrow, and the crew must be at their stations."

"But—"

"No." Ash didn't raise his voice, but his tone was utterly final.

Dai gave Chase a sympathetic glance and a slight shrug. It was clear he wasn't going to go against his Commander's orders.

Chase crossed his arms, slouching back in his chair. "Well, *I'm* not going to be on call," he snapped at Ash. "I'll be busy with the race. You'll have to find someone else to drive the truck."

"Chase," Killian hissed. "Do you *want* to get yourself fired?"

The Commander made a slight, gracious motion with one hand, brushing aside Chase's rudeness. "Given the circumstances, I can extend Chase some leeway. But I too have superiors, and they are starting to ask questions about my driver. Chase, I have managed to keep you off the duty roster during the air race, citing extraordinary personal circumstances, but you *must* be available immediately afterwards. I cannot cover for your absences any further than that."

Chase drummed his fingers on the tabletop. "You won't have to," he said abruptly. "Because I'm quitting."

"*What?*" Hugh and Dai exclaimed together.

Ash's neutral expression didn't change, but he went very still. "Chase, please do not make a decision in haste."

Chase shook his head, his jaw set stubbornly. "You say that our responsibilities to the city have to come first. Not for me. My mate has to come first, every time."

"Of course everyone here understands that, Chase," Virginia said, touching his hand lightly. "But you can't just quit. The team needs you. And besides, you *love* being a firefighter."

"After all, where else can you get paid for driving like a lunatic?" Dai added, his tone light but his green eyes deeply concerned.

"Ah, who cares about all that?" Chase waved a hand airily. "It's not like I need the job. All I have to do is call my dad, and I'm CEO-in-training of Tiernach Enterprises. Right, Killian?"

"Your father will be thrilled," Killian said, though he himself looked extremely un-thrilled at the prospect of working for his cousin. "He's always hoped that you'd grow out of your reckless phase and take your rightful place in the family business."

"Right. Can't play with cars and planes forever." Chase straightened up, copying Killian's formal, business-like pose. "And I've got to think about providing for my mate, after all. Financial services pays a lot better than merely saving lives."

Despite his flippant words, Connie could tell how much his resignation had actually cost him. His shoulders were set in a tight, unhappy line.

"You don't have to do this for me," she said to him quietly.

He met her eyes levelly, his own utterly serious. "Yes, I do. I'm not losing you again. Whatever happens, wherever you go, I'm going too."

Connie bristled. "Don't I get a say in that?"

His mouth quirked. "Well, you get to decide whether I'm in your bed or pining after you from a distance, but other than that... no, not really."

"I'm afraid that really is how shifters are, when it comes to our mates," Dai said, with a quick, tender glance at Virginia. "Once you've met her, that's it. There'll never be anyone else for you, ever."

Connie folded her arms. "That's not my experience."

Chase flinched. "That's why I brought you here. I want you to talk to Dai and Virginia about being mated, while I'm busy with Sammy. Please? It was difficult for them at first too."

"I know how strange it is to us ordinary humans." Virginia smiled sympathetically at Connie. "So I think I might be able to explain things better than Chase can."

"A *parrot* can explain things better than Chase can," Hugh muttered.

"Hugh, on the other hand, can't stand being touched and hates all of humanity. This does not make him a good source of relationship advice," Chase told Connie as he stood up. "But he will protect you, along with Dai. And Killian, too. You'll be safe here."

Dai's eyes flashed fiery gold for a second. "No mere wyvern will get past me. I can promise you that."

Chase clapped him on the shoulder, then looked back at Ash. "I was going to ask for your help with Sammy Smiles. But given the circumstances…"

"Even if I will no longer be your Commander," the Phoenix said, rising, "I will always be your friend. How can I assist?"

Chase grinned, though his usual bright sparkle was subdued. "You can eat dinner."

CHAPTER 12

Chase found Sammy Smiles enjoying a lobster dinner at an upmarket waterside restaurant overlooking the Brighton Marina.

Or rather, he *was* enjoying his dinner, until Chase walked in and punched him right in the face.

The maître d'hôtel squawked in outrage, while half a dozen shark shifters scattered through the restaurant shot to their feet. Two tiger sharks seized Chase's arms in crushing grips.

"Well, that sure makes my life easier," Sammy said, dabbing at his bleeding nose with a napkin. "Thanks, son. You're going to be watching the air race from a jail cell. *If* you're lucky."

From the doorway, Commander Ash cleared his throat softly.

The two shifters holding Chase's arms abruptly let go. Another shark shifter hastily blew out the lit candle decorating the dining table.

"Commander Ash." Sammy's eyes narrowed. "What an unexpected pleasure. Can't see any fires here, though."

The Commander gave him a courteous nod, then turned to the flustered maître d'. "Table for one, please."

The maître d' dithered, looking from Ash to Sammy. "Er... shall I call the police, sir?"

"No need. Just a little misunderstanding," Sammy told him. He stared hard at Chase. "Pull up a chair, son. You've got my attention."

I believe that I should remind you that I am forbidden from burning them, even if they become violent. Commander Ash sent telepathically to Chase, so that the sharks couldn't hear. *Under the terms of my asylum, as granted by the Parliament of Shifters, I may only use my powers against other shifters if they commit arson.*

I know that, Chase sent back as he seated himself at Sammy's table. *And I'm pretty sure Sammy knows that, too.*

Commander Ash appeared to be completely focused on his menu. *Then I fail to see how my presence can act as a deterrent.*

Chase grinned, watching the shark shifters. They were all eyeing the Commander as though he was a ticking time bomb. The Phoenix was such a stickler for following the rules, it never even occurred to him that other people could worry that he *might* break them.

I know you don't, he sent to Ash. *Trust me. Try the shrimp, it's excellent.*

"So, son." Sammy leaned back in his chair, his eyes suspicious above his gleaming smile. "What's this about?"

"You know very well." Chase's own smile sharpened, showing his teeth. "You tried to kill my mate."

Sammy spread his stubby hands. "Pretty certain I haven't tried to kill anyone, let alone your mate. I don't even know who the lucky lady is."

"Oh, but you do." Chase's rage burned in his blood. His pegasus was desperate to trample Sammy into a bloody pulp. "Shane West's daughter, Constance. She was flying his Spitfire when your hired assassin attacked. It's only thanks to me that she isn't at the bottom of the sea along with the plane."

The front legs of Sammy's chair crashed down. "My Spitfire is *where*?"

"Don't play the innocent with me," Chase snarled. "Bad news, Sammy. It takes a lot more than a wyvern to knock me out of the sky."

The Great White shark shifter stared at him, to all appearances genuinely baffled. "Son, I haven't the faintest idea what you're rattling on about."

This is why I really needed Griff...

If Griff had been here, they would have been able to get Sammy arrested—the shifter police force knew Griff well enough to act on his testimony without hesitation. But without the half-eagle shifter's special ability, Chase had no way of proving that Sammy was lying.

Just got to keep charging ahead. Keep Sammy off-balance, in the hopes he'll trip up.

"I know it was you," Chase said. "You're the only one with a motive. And I have iron-clad proof that you hired that wyvern."

"You'll regret it if you try to catch me with fake evidence, son. My lawyer is a real shark." Sammy rubbed his chin, his expression unreadable. "Wyvern, you say? Boys, do any of you know a wyvern shifter?"

A general murmur of "No, boss" ran around the table, as Sammy's goons shook their heads.

"Pity." Sammy snapped a claw off his lobster. "I'm suddenly real eager to make one's acquaintance."

A couple of Sammy's goons quietly got up, abandoning their half-eaten dinners. With the speed of sharks following a blood-trail, they headed out the door.

Gone to find the wyvern... to warn it?

Chase knew that the wyvern wasn't in Brighton at the moment—his pegasus senses covered the entire city, and there was no hint of the wyvern's distinctive scent. But Sammy knew of his ability. No doubt he'd told his hired assassin to stay out of Chase's range.

He was tempted to follow the shifters immediately, in the hopes that they would lead him to the wyvern. But he wasn't finished with Sammy yet.

Yes, his stallion told him. *Fight this one, kill him, now! He threatened our mate!*

Sammy appeared not to have noticed his henchmen's departure. "You say this wyvern knocked the Spitfire down into the drink, son?"

"That's right," Chase said, trying to ignore his stallion's bloodlust. "And if you try to steal it, you'll get a big surprise."

"I remember your sea dragon friend. So he's guarding my plane. That's real neighborly of him." Sammy waved the lobster claw at one of his remaining thugs. "Send the nice dragon a fruit basket from me, will you?"

"It's not *your* plane," Chase snapped. "And it's not going to be."

"Well now." Sammy leaned back again. "Seems to me that it is. The bet's that West's Spitfire will win the Rydon Cup. Even a hotshot pegasus is going to have a mite of trouble winning a race with a plane that's underwater."

Gotcha!

"Thank you, Sammy." Chase stood up. "That's *exactly* what I needed to hear you say. West's Spitfire will win the Rydon Cup, I can promise you that. And I can promise you one other thing."

"And what might that be, son?" Sammy's eyebrows rose.

Chase leaned on the table, staring Sammy straight in the eye. "If you ever, *ever* try to harm my mate again, in any way, no matter how indirectly, I will find you. I will hunt you down wherever you try to hide, and then I will personally kick your teeth out through your asshole."

The shark shifters to either side of Chase bristled, then hesitated. They glanced over at Commander Ash, who was peacefully buttering a bread roll.

"No need, boys." Sammy waved his shifters back down again. "It's understandable that our pegasus friend here is mite het up, seeing as how some pond scum has been threatening his mate. I'm willing to cut him a little slack."

Casually, Sammy popped the lobster claw into his mouth. The thick shell splintered as the shark shifter bit down.

"A *little* slack," Sammy said, pulling the cracked claw out of his mouth. He idly started picking out bits of lobster meat. "I'm as pained as you are, son, I really am. To think of that beautiful plane all tangled up in seaweed… it breaks my heart. I sure would like to have words with the kind of monster that would ruin a noble warbird like that. You let me know if you find this wyvern shifter, you hear?"

"Oh, don't worry," Chase said. "I will."

CHAPTER 13

"And that's how we met," Virginia concluded. She exchanged a long, warm look with Dai, their intertwined hands resting on the top of the table.

Connie felt a little embarrassed to be watching them, like she was intruding on their privacy. There was a deep, unspoken intimacy between the pair that made her feel like a spare wheel. From the way Killian had apparently become fascinated by something at the other end of the bar, he felt just as awkward.

"If you're going to stare at each other like that, for God's sake, get a room," Hugh snapped. He had his back pressed to the wall, as far from Dai and Virginia as he could get without being on the other side of it. "You've already spoken quite long enough about the joys of being mated. No need to provide us with a physical demonstration as well."

Connie couldn't help but notice that the paramedic was keeping a marked distance from her, too. When they'd left the private room to head to the more comfortable main bar area, she'd accidentally brushed against Hugh going down the stairs. He'd jerked away from her touch as if she was radioactive. At least he seemed to have the same distaste for Dai and Virginia as well. The only person he didn't seem to mind being near was Killian, oddly.

Virginia just smiled, clearly well used to ignoring Hugh's surly attitude. "So, any questions?" she asked Connie.

Connie had a hunch that there was a lot more to the story than Virginia had revealed. "I don't mean to pry, but... did you ever doubt your feelings for each other?"

One corner of Virginia's mouth curved upward. "Well, I did flee from him in terror one time."

"Believe me, my mate is very kindly painting me in a much better light than I deserve," Dai said wryly. "I was so cautious when it came to telling her the truth about myself, I very nearly lost everything. I'm glad Chase hasn't made *that* mistake, at least."

"Not talking enough," Killian muttered, "has never been one of Chase's problems."

"But *you* never doubted your feelings for Virginia," Connie said to Dai.

"Never," the dragon shifter said, with utter conviction. "One you meet your mate, that's it. You just know, bone-deep, that there's no one else for you."

"And that's the way that Chase feels about you," Virginia added, smiling at Connie.

Connie scowled down into her drink. "That's how he *says* he feels."

Killian shot her a sidelong glance. "Could I ask you something?" he said to Dai. "Does Chase have a... reputation?"

"Chase has a *lot* of reputations," Dai said, his tone dry. "Were you thinking of anything in particular?"

Killian sighed. "A reputation when it comes to women."

Of course. He knows why I left Chase.

Killian had been the one who'd called Connie on that horrible morning, three years ago, to ask if she knew where his cousin was. He'd always had to look out for Chase, the same way she'd always had to rescue her dad from *his* drunken mishaps.

Killian had begged her to go make sure that Chase had gotten home safely, so sincerely that Connie had swallowed her hurt pride at being stood up and done so. And so she'd walked in on Chase in the aftermath of one of his infamous one-night-stands... the ones that he'd sworn he'd given up.

And if she really was his mate, he *should* have given them up, without hesitation or a second thought.

"Sorry, Connie," Killian added, throwing her an apologetic look. "But Virginia's story has made it clear that it's best if everyone knows the truth."

"No, that's all right. I want to know too." She turned back to Dai. "You can be honest."

From the conflicted expression on the dragon shifter's face, he really, *really* didn't want to be honest.

"If you know Chase at all, you know that he does everything at top speed and with excessive enthusiasm," Virginia said. She shrugged. "As far as I'm aware, that includes his love life. But does it matter what he's done in the past? *You're* his future."

"That's right," Dai said, shooting his mate a grateful look for rescuing him. "As a shifter, I can promise you that Chase will be true to you. You're his mate. He'll never look at another woman again, now that he's met you."

Killian's mouth tightened. "Chase met Connie three years ago."

Connie avoided Dai and Virginia's shocked stares. Hot humiliation rose in her cheeks. She stared down at the table, unable to speak past the tight pain closing her throat.

"That's not possible," Dai said blankly.

"My cousin is the most impossible person in the world," Killian said, sounding resigned. "But I didn't think that even he could break something as sacred as the mate-bond. Connie, I'm so, so sorry. You're a good person, and you deserve better. It's not your fault."

Maybe it is.

I'm too cautious, I could never bring myself to trust him fully. Maybe we would have had a beautiful, perfect bond, just like Dai and Virginia, if only I hadn't held back.

Maybe it is all my fault.

Connie angrily scrubbed her knuckles across her eyes, dashing away the tears before they could spill. "It's nothing to me," she said defiantly. "*I'm* not a shifter, after all. *I* don't have some amazing instant connection that means he's the only man for me. Chase can sleep around as much as he wants, for all I care."

"Chase doesn't sleep around," Hugh said. For the first time, he didn't sound even slightly sarcastic. "He hasn't for as long as I've known him."

"It's good of you to try to defend your friend," Killian said to him. "But please, don't lie to Connie. She's been hurt enough already."

Hugh rubbed at his forehead as if he had a headache. "I can't believe I'm doing this," he muttered, apparently to himself. "One mated pair around here is bad enough..."

He dropped his hand again with a sigh, looking at Connie. "If you're going to refuse Chase, do it for something he's actually done, not something he hasn't. Take my word on it, he's not slept with anyone for at least three years. He hasn't even lusted after anyone."

Dai was looking at the paramedic in fascination, as though he'd never heard him talk like this before. "But Chase is *always* flirting with women."

"No, he's just being himself. The same way he is with everyone, male or female." Hugh shrugged. "He's charming and charismatic, and women mistake that for interest and throw themselves at him. But he never takes them up on it."

"How can you be so sure?" Connie asked him, suspiciously.

"Healing is my useful talent." Hugh sipped his drink, hiding his expression. "Not my only one."

"You know, this *would* explain why no one ever asks Chase to walk them home twice," Virginia said thoughtfully. "And why the women always look terribly disappointed afterwards. I just assumed he was an awful lover."

"Evidently not," Hugh muttered, flashing a sidelong glance at Connie.

Connie couldn't stop the blush from rising up her face again... or the hope from rising up in her heart.

Maybe it is true. Maybe Chase really hasn't played around since he met me. Maybe he can't. Maybe I really am his—

She realized that Killian was studying her. He touched her arm. "Can I talk to you for a moment?"

Connie let Killian draw her a little to one side, out of earshot of the others. "Do *you* think it's true?" she asked him.

"I can't say that I do." He blew out his breath, shaking his head. "I want to think the best of my cousin, I really do, but... I know him. He's never been able to keep it in his pants for three days, let alone three years."

Connie's heart plummeted like her plane. "But, what if Hugh really can tell whether someone's been chaste?"

"I've never heard of any sort of shifter who can do that. I think Hugh is just trying to protect his friend. Connie, you're the one who caught Chase cheating on you. You saw it with your own eyes." Killian spread his hands, palm up. "Do you *really* think nothing happened? It just doesn't sound very believable to me."

Chase said nothing happened...

But he would say that, wouldn't he?

"You're right," she said dully.

"Of course he's right," said a cheerful voice. "Killian is always right. You should definitely listen to him."

Connie spun around to see Chase grinning at them. He was a little out of breath, as if he'd been flying hard and had only just walked in.

"As long as he's only been saying nice things about me, of course." Chase's smile faltered as he looked at her face. "Connie? What's wrong?"

"Nothing." Connie shook him off as he tried to take her hand. "Just been talking to your friends. I hope your conversation with Sammy was more productive."

"I got what I needed, though not everything I'd hoped for." Chase reached out to her again, but she stepped away. "Connie, what—?"

"I don't want to talk about it." Connie hugged herself, glaring at him. "I've wasted enough time already. What about my plane, Chase? That's all that matters. How am I going to save my plane from Sammy?"

"But—" Chase started.

"For once in your life, *drop it,*" Killian told him. "Seriously. What's your plan?"

Chase looked rebellious, but allowed the change of topic. "The same as before, of course. We're going to win the race in Connie's Spitfire."

"My Spitfire is underwater, Chase," Connie snapped. "Even if your sea dragon friend can get it out, there is no way it's flying anytime soon."

Chase's grin reappeared. "Sammy just said *West's Spitfire* had to win the race. He didn't specify which one."

Connie stared at him. "Are you seriously suggesting that we go out and buy another Spitfire?"

"Oh no." Killian held up his hands, palm out and fingers spread. "Chase, I can't liquidate assets on a moment's notice. I don't have the ready cash for this sort of purchase."

"Even if you did, it wouldn't do any good," Connie told him. "You can't just buy a Spitfire off eBay. They only come up for sale once in a blue moon!"

"I know that. In fact, I know that better than you do." Chase stuck his hands in his pockets, gazing contemplatively up at the ceiling. "Killian, you remember that money you lent me a little while ago?"

"Strangely, I do indeed remember advancing you several million pounds," Killian said dryly. "It's the sort of thing that sticks in my memory. Why?"

Chase looked insufferably smug. "I think it's time to show you what I bought."

CHAPTER 14

Now this was definitely *worth two and a half million dollars,* Chase thought, delighted by the matching dumbfounded expressions on Killian and Connie's faces as they stared at his plane.

The single-seater Mark IX Spitfire dominated the small private hanger he'd rented. Chase was glad of all the hours he'd spent lovingly polishing the plane's sleek curves. It shone like a vast precious gem, light sparkling from the immaculate paintwork. If they'd been in private, he would have been tempted to try proposing to Connie with it.

"When did you buy a Spitfire?" Connie said at last, weakly. "More to the point, *why* did you buy a Spitfire?"

"I told you." Chase raised an eyebrow at her, unable to control his wide smirk. "Whenever I saw something that reminded me of you, I had to get it."

Killian shook his head, his expression half-amused, half-despairing. "And I thought you needed the money to pay off gambling debts. Well, I suppose that there are worse investments. At least you should be able to resell it in future at a profit."

"Sorry, coz, but no." Chase pulled the Spitfire's registration papers out of his jacket, casually handing them to Connie. "Because it's not my plane anymore."

Connie looked down at the paperwork, then back up at him in disbelief. "You cannot be serious."

"The bet is on West's Spitfire winning the race. Sammy said so himself." Chase pointed first at Connie, then at the plane. "You're West, and now this is your Spitfire. So you can still win the bet."

"*How* much did you say this plane was worth?" Killian's voice had gone high and strangled.

"Two and a half million dollars, give or take a bit." Chase patted him on the shoulder. "Relax, Killian. It's only money."

"I promise, I won't keep it," Connie said to Killian. "As soon as the race is over, I'll give it straight back."

Killian pulled at his dark hair, his gray eyes rather wild. "Do neither of you understand capital gains? This is a very tax-inefficient plan! And what happens if you don't win the race? Does Sammy get to keep both Spitfires?"

Chase shrugged carelessly. "I suppose so. I hadn't really thought about it. We're not going to lose the race, after all."

Connie walked around the plane, scrutinizing every inch with an expert eye. "Well, she certainly looks to be in good repair. I can give her a last-minute tune-up to make sure she's at peak performance. But Chase, are you really sure you can do this?"

"What do you mean?" he asked.

"She's a standard single-seater fighter." Connie pointed up at the cockpit. "Not a two-seater trainer plane like mine. I won't be able to navigate for you. Are you really going to be able to learn the route by tomorrow? Well enough to fly it unaided?"

"Not a chance," Chase said, honestly. "But I'm not going to be piloting. You are."

Connie went white. "I'm *what?*"

"Good-bye, two and a half million dollars," Killian muttered.

Chase kicked the side of his cousin's foot. "Don't underestimate my mate. She knows the course so well, she could fly it in her sleep. She can do this."

"No, I really can't!" Connie yelped. "Chase, you have to fly. You're the one with magic powers!"

"Which means I have to be outside the plane, ready to protect you from the wyvern," Chase said firmly. "I'm certain it's going to come back. I can't fly in the race and evade it at the same time. But I *can* fight it in pegasus form. I can hold it off long enough for you to win."

Connie looked desperately at Killian. "Couldn't you guard Chase while he races?"

"Me?" Killian took a sharp step back, looking dismayed. "I'm not as crazy as my cousin. I'd have to be suicidal to try to take on a wyvern single-handed. Though I'm not going to let *him* take one on by himself, either. I'll back you up, Chase."

"I knew I didn't even have to ask." Chase bumped him affectionately, shoulder to shoulder. "And don't run yourself down. Even if you spend most of your time behind a desk, you're still a pegasus, and a Tiernach. You're tougher than you realize. Just like Connie."

"I'm not." Connie swung her head from side to side in vigorous denial. "I can't, Chase. I can't do it. I'm not as good a pilot as you."

"No. You're not." He caught her chin in his hand, holding her still and forcing her to look at him. "You're a *better* pilot than me. I couldn't have pulled your Spitfire out of that death-spiral, but you did. The only thing that's ever held you back is your sense of caution. You just have to be willing to take a few risks."

"I'll lose, I'll lose my plane, and it will be all my fault," Connie said, her voice rising. She reminded him of a cornered animal, lashing out in fear. "It'll be *your* fault for making me do this. I'll never be able to look at you again."

"You aren't going to lose." With all his heart, Chase wished that they were truly mated, so that she could feel his bone-deep confidence in her. "Please, Connie. Trust—"

"Don't you dare tell me to trust you," Connie snarled at him. "Not again. Not *ever* again."

"That's not what I was going to say," Chase said, with perfect truth. He stared deep into her frightened eyes, willing her to believe him, just this once. "Connie. Trust *yourself*."

CHAPTER 15

I can't do this.

Connie felt physically sick with nerves, her stomach clenching around the small breakfast Chase had forced her to eat. An excited crowd was gathering around the edges of the airfield, eagerly waiting for the race to start. Connie tried to concentrate on her plane, but it was hard to ignore the way people kept pointing at her and the Spitfire. The back of her neck burned under the heat of hundreds of curious stares.

"That's everything on the pre-flight checklist," Chase said, ducking under the nose of the plane to rejoin her. "As soon as we get the signal, you'll be cleared for take off. Are you ready?"

"No." Connie's hands were shaking so badly, she couldn't even do up her flight jacket. "Chase, I can't do this."

"Here." Chase carefully fastened her zip for her. "There you go. All set."

"I mean, I can't fly this race!"

"I know what you meant." Chase brushed a stray strand of her hair out of her face, tucking it behind her ear. "And you can. Your practice run earlier was perfect. You comfortably beat everyone else's time."

"That was just the practice run, with a clear sky. It'll be different with the other planes up there too. What if I can't get past the leaders? What if I make a mistake? What if—"

"Connie. You can do this. Just—" Chase cut himself off, his back stiffening. "What is he doing here?"

Connie followed the direction of his gaze, and her heart leapt with anxiety. "Oh God, this is really happening. It's the race marshal. He must be coming to give us permission to take off."

"Not him," Chase said grimly. He was staring hard at an enormous man in a brilliant white suit who was sauntering alongside the approaching marshal. "*Him*. That's Sammy Smiles."

Even if Connie hadn't known Sammy was a shifter, she would have thought there was something odd about his bizarrely top-heavy physique and impossibly wide, toothy mouth. Knowing what he truly was, she recognized them as the unmistakable traits of his other form. He looked more like a shark stuffed into a suit than a human being.

He also looked very, very pleased with himself.

"Ms. West?" the marshal said, consulting his clipboard as he came up to them. "Are your pre-flight checks complete?"

Chase thrust the paperwork at the marshal without looking, never breaking eye contact with Sammy. "You're not welcome here, Sammy. Get back behind the line with the other spectators."

The marshal coughed disapprovingly. "Mr. Smiles, as our *very* generous sponsor, is personally wishing all the pilots the best of luck before take off."

A minute ago, Connie wouldn't have thought that she could possibly feel any *more* sick. "You sponsor the Rydon Cup?"

"Why, didn't I mention that before?" Sammy drawled in a thick Texan accent. He beamed at her, showing double rows of sharp teeth. "And you must be West's daughter. Aren't you just a sweet little thing. Why, who'd have thought such soft, pretty hands could possibly manage to fly a big ol' plane like this?"

No doubt he'd been intending to psych her out... but his underhanded insult had the opposite effect. She was used to patronizing older men trying to tell her how to look after a plane, as if she hadn't cut her teeth on a torque wrench. The butterflies in her stomach turned into angry bees.

"I flew my first Spitfire when I was seven," she spat, clenching her fists. "Sitting on my mom's lap. You'll find that I know what I'm doing."

Chase's chest swelled with pride, his eyes shining with fierce delight as he glanced at her. "Oh, Sammy. You're about to find out that you've jumped out of the frying pan and into the inferno. By the end of today, you are really, really going to regret that you prevented *me* from piloting."

A wounded expression spread across Sammy's broad face. "Now, now. I haven't prevented anyone from doing anything. And if you keep making these accusations, son, I'm going to have to insist you speak to my lawyer. But let's not be unfriendly. We all need to put any little differences aside and be good sports. We want a nice, clean race, don't we?"

Connie noticed that Sammy looked hard at Chase as he said this last bit. She realized that the shark shifter was worried that Chase, in pegasus form, might take it upon himself to interfere with the other planes.

"Cheaters always think that everyone else cheats too." Chase matched Sammy's smile, baring his teeth. "But we're not like you, Sammy. Connie is going to win this race fair and square."

Sammy gazed up at the plane. "Speaking of a fair race..." he trailed off, glancing at the race marshal meaningfully.

"Ah, yes." The marshal, who had been looking rather confused by the hostile undertones to the conversation, straightened up. "Ms. West, due to the unfortunate malfunction on your other Spitfire, we've accepted this rather unconventional last-minute substitution. But, after careful consideration, we have decided that we must adjust your handicap."

Connie had been expecting something like this. As a handicap race, all the planes in the Rydon Cup started at different times, so that it became a test of pilot skill rather than just the plane's raw capabilities. Previously, Connie had been set to start in sixth position, out of a field of twelve.

But Chase's Spitfire—she still couldn't think of it as *hers*—was a fair bit lighter than hers, thanks to only carrying a single person rather than two. It would be fractionally faster in the sky as a result, and therefore needed a bigger handicap.

"Now, wait a second—" Chase began.

Connie stopped him with an upraised hand. "No, it's only fair. So I'm starting in seventh place now, marshal?"

"Er, after impartial review and consideration of some new evidence..." The marshal's eyes flicked briefly to Sammy. "You will be starting in twelfth position."

Connie stared at him in utter horror. *"Dead last?"*

Chase towered over the smaller man, his muscular shoulders bunching ominously. "Let me guess. Did this 'new evidence' come in the form of a fat check, by any chance?"

The marshal held his clipboard in front of him like a shield, visibly paling. "The—the decision of the committee is final," he gabbled. "Please prepare for take off, and await your starting signal."

"This is a real nice plane." Sammy patted the Spitfire affectionately. "I sure am looking forward to spending more time with her in the future. Nice to meet you, Constance West. Oh, and tell your dad that if he needs a little loan to tide you over after this... he knows where to find me."

"That's it," Connie said, as Sammy sauntered off, whistling. "It's over."

Chase looked as if he could quite happily have murdered the loan shark on the spot. "It is *not* over," he said fiercely. "You said it yourself —you've been flying these planes all your life. You can do this, Connie. Don't think about what you've got to lose. Focus on what you're going to *win*. Think how much you want to rub Sammy's smile in the dirt. Think how satisfying it's going to be to see his face when you come in first."

Connie groped for her earlier flare of rage, but her common sense smothered it. "I'm a good pilot, but I'm not a daredevil like my dad. Overtaking other planes is risky, and I'll have to do it eleven times!"

"Then take those risks." Chase seized her hands, squeezing them in a crushing grip. "Let yourself go, fly like you were born in the sky. This plane has survived me flinging it around, after all. It's not going to come apart around you. And I'm going to be right there at your wingtip. I won't let anything happen to you."

"But—" Connie started.

He leaned down and kissed her, fiercely, deeply, stifling any further protests. Heat ran through Connie's blood. She felt as if his wild energy was spilling from him into her, rekindling the fire in her belly. She pressed against him, as if she could draw his reckless courage into herself, storing it up for the race ahead.

Chase drew back a little, leaning his forehead against hers. "You can do this," he repeated. "I'll see you in the sky, and I'll make sure you can see me too."

Connie clung onto his hands, afraid that once he let go, all her courage would leak away like a deflating balloon. "If you can drive off the wyvern, will you come and fly the race with me? Please?"

"I'll be right by your side, I swear." He gave her one last brief, tantalizing kiss. "Now go. It's time."

CHAPTER 16

Chase could sense the wyvern approaching. He'd barely slept last night, waiting for the shifter to return to the city, but it had only appeared at the edge of his perception as the planes took off for the race. It was still too high and distant to be seen, but it was closing in fast.

Incoming, he telepathically sent to Killian. He accompanied the thought with a mental image of the wyvern's green form, so that Killian's pegasus would be able to get its scent and track it too. *You ready?*

To fight a wyvern? Not even remotely. Despite his words, Killian's wide gray wings beat steadily, his flight smooth and strong as he circled over the racing planes. *I can sense it now, too. Looks like it's planning to intercept over the sea, during the later stage of the race.*

I agree. Chase increased his wingbeats, quickening his pace. *I'm going to see if I can catch it before it gets a chance to interfere with the race. You keep back here with Connie, just in case.*

He couldn't resist glancing down at the race as he powered through the sky. Thanks to Sammy's fiddling with the handicaps, five of the eleven planes that had started ahead of Connie were technically faster than the vintage Spitfire. But that didn't mean that they were faster in practice. A plane was only as good as its pilot.

Connie had already overtaken the plane that had started eleventh, when its pilot had run into some crosswinds at takeoff. Now she was closing rapidly on the next one, the Spitfire's engine roaring at full throttle. She'd taken advantage of the Spitfire's superior climbing ability to get above the light acrobatic plane. The modern plane might be faster in level flight, but not in a dive. All she needed was an opening.

The other aircraft took the turn a little sloppily, wavering from the ideal racing line... just a little.

Now, Connie, now! Be bold!

As if she'd heard his silent exhortation, the Spitfire flashed downward. Its wings sliced through the air like a knife through butter as Connie wheeled it neatly through the turn, cutting ahead of the other plane.

Yes! Two down!

Only nine more to go...

He desperately wanted to fly wingtip-to-wingtip with Connie through the race, sharing in her triumph, but he had a job to do. The racing planes became just distant glints as he flew out to sea at full speed.

Do you have a plan, by the way? Killian sent to him, his mental voice a little faint with distance.

Yes, Chase replied, the wind whistling past his flattened ears. *I'm going to find the bastard who tried to kill my mate, and I'm going to kick his fucking head in.*

There was no further time for talking. He could see the wyvern now. It was a little lower down than him, flying close to the sea. Its long, jagged wings beat steadily, propelling it at incredible speed.

Kill! His pegasus filled his mind with a single-minded need to smash the wyvern out of the sky. *No one attacks our mate! Kill!*

Shrieking in challenge, Chase folded his wings and stooped. The wyvern's wedge-shape head whipped round, its large, acid-yellow eyes widening in alarm as it spotted him. Its narrow chest swelled. It spat out a cloud of acid.

Chase flicked a pinion, swooping around the deadly mist. He lashed out at the wyvern with his razor-sharp front hooves. It twisted its sinuous body, evading his kick. He didn't give it a chance to recover, striking out at it with both teeth and hooves.

If I stay close, it can't use its acid. Just got to watch out for the tail.

The wyvern's deadly, scorpion-like tail curved over its back, the needle sharp tip swinging to target him. Chase was so busy keeping an eye on it that he nearly forgot that the front half of the wyvern was just as dangerous. Its head darted at him, fangs gleaming with poison.

Chase backwinged hard, nearly stalling out as the wyvern's teeth snapped shut on empty air. Off balance, he couldn't avoid the wyvern's tail as it whipped round. It didn't manage to sting him, but the powerful blow still sent him tumbling across the sky.

The wyvern didn't press its advantage. Instead, it increased its wingbeats, shooting away from him like a bullet out of a gun. Although the wyvern's deadly acid and poisonous tail made it more than a match for a pegasus, it didn't seem to be interested in a fight. Chase guessed that Sammy had ordered it to evade him and head straight for the race, to make sure Connie didn't win.

Recovering himself, Chase shot after the wyvern. It twisted its neck, breathing out a couple more blasts of acid to cover its retreat. Chase banked round the drifting clouds in tight, swooping arcs, locked onto the wyvern like a heat-seeking missile, but every evasive maneuver cost him precious time.

The wyvern's long wings boomed with every stroke, propelling it away from him at a phenomenal pace. Chase's powerful flight muscles burned as he tried to keep up. Even at the very limits of his speed, the wyvern was creeping away from him.

The planes are heading out to sea. Killian's anxious mental voice burst into his head. *They'll be nearing you soon. Connie's worked her way up to sixth position. Are you okay? Do you need help?*

Stay with the race! Chase flung back, his psychic voice as out-of-breath as his physical body. He needed Killian there as a last-ditch defense, if worst came to worst.

Chase bared his teeth in a frustrated snarl as the wyvern inched yet farther away. No matter how he pushed himself, he couldn't catch up. He had more strength and endurance, but the wyvern was simply faster in level flight than he was. It only needed to maintain its speed for a few more minutes before it would be in the midst of the air race.

What would Connie do...?

He altered the angle of his wings, striving to gain height rather than speed. The wyvern dropped away beneath him, pulling ahead. Its wedge-shaped head swiveled on its long, sinuous neck as it tried to work out where he'd gone. Borrowing a trick from WWII fighter pilots, Chase headed straight for the sun, hiding in the dazzling rays as he climbed even higher.

He could see the racing planes now, and hear the air-shaking thunder of their combined engines. Connie's Spitfire was immediately apparent, a predatory hawk-shape amidst the smaller light aircraft. A group of RV-7s scattered in disarray as she roared straight through their midst.

The wyvern's head swung, locking onto the Spitfire. It soared up on an intercept course.

He's attacking our mate! His pegasus was frantic. *Protect! Strike! Kill!*

Chase fought for control, struggling to resist the pegasus's overwhelming instinct to immediately dive after the wyvern. He was usually so in tune with his stallion that it felt unnatural to go against its desires.

But for once, he had to keep a cool head. Rushing in too quickly would result in disaster.

Wait, he told the stallion. *Wait! We're only going to get one shot at this!*

The wyvern was too fast and agile for him. He knew that his only chance was to dive at terminal velocity, falling so fast that even the wyvern's hair-trigger reflexes wouldn't be able to evade him. But to do that, he had to get higher.

Now, Killian! he sent to his cousin, as he clawed his way upward. *Delay it!*

Killian swooped at the wyvern. The wyvern shook him off, easily dodging the attacks. It had reached the race corridor now. It avoided a couple of planes, allowing them to pass unhindered, then hovered, waiting. Killian darted at its head like a crow mobbing a bird of prey, but the wyvern just blasted acid at him, forcing him to veer away.

I can't get close! Killian sent to him in dismay. *It's right in Connie's path, and I can't get it to budge.*

Just distract it as much as you can, Chase sent back.

Air burned like fire in his nostrils, his great lungs heaving with exertion as he struggled through the dead air. There was no updraft, no thermal to carry him upward. It was like trying to climb a sheer cliff with his bare hands.

You can't dive from that high! Killian's mental voice was horrified. *You'll break your neck!*

He ignored his cousin's warning, heaving himself up even further. He was so high now that the planes beneath him looked as small as children's toys. Killian was just a gray speck, whirling round the stationary, bright green dot of the wyvern.

Chase! It's too—I can't—! Killian's psychic message broke apart into a wordless impression of pain.

Chase's laboring heart missed a beat as he saw his cousin's distant form tumble down toward the waves. To his relief, Killian pulled up before he hit the water, but from his wavering, unsteady course, it was clear he was out of the fight.

Connie neatly cut off another plane, flying the twists and turns of the race route with cool, considered efficiency. She was in third place now, but she had a huge distance to make up in order to catch the two race leaders. The Spitfire surged forward as Connie gave it full throttle.

Heading straight toward the waiting wyvern.

Connie had no way of knowing the beast was there. Secure in its invisibility, the wyvern hovered directly in her path. All of its attention was focused on the approaching plane.

NOW!

Chase swept his wings back, folding them tight to his sides. Flying on just the barest tips of his pinions, he flashed downward. His tail streamed out behind him like a banner as he picked up speed, falling faster and faster until he felt like his wings were going to be torn off.

The howling wind lashed his face so hard that it was impossible to draw breath. Black spots danced in his vision as his lungs burned for air. He twisted his wings, swinging round as he fell, hooves ready to strike.

At the very last instant, the wyvern suddenly threw itself to one side, as if someone had shouted a warning at it. But it was too late. Chase was diving so fast that even the wyvern's supernaturally fast reflexes couldn't save it.

All four of his hooves hit the wyvern's flank, the bone-jarring impact nearly making him black out. If he'd hit the wyvern's head, he would have instantly broken its neck. As it was, the beast bowled head-over-tail, spinning uncontrollably down toward the water.

Still dizzy from the dive, Chase was nearly knocked out of the air himself as Connie's Spitfire shot past him with barely a foot to spare. He was tossed helplessly in the wind from the plane's wake, bobbing like a cork on a stormy sea.

By the time he'd righted himself, the wyvern was half-way back to Brighton, abandoning the fight. It flew low to the sea, its wing-beats erratic and labored as it fled.

Follow it! His pegasus pawed the air, eager to finish off the beast. *Catch it, kill it, stomp it flat!*

Chase shook his head to dispel his stallion's instinctive bloodlust. *No,* he told his pegasus. *We have to help our mate. We promised to be there at her wingtip. And we will* never *again break a promise to her, ever.*

He forced his aching wings to beat faster, catching up with the Spitfire. Despite his burning muscles, he fell into formation with the plane.

I'm here, Connie. And now, it's all up to you.

CHAPTER 17

I'm going to lose.

Connie forced her hands to stay steady on the controls. She didn't have the luxury of shaking now. Her eyes stayed locked onto the two race leaders.

They were both modified Mudry CAP 230 aircraft, a high-speed acrobatics plane favored by serious racing pilots. Her own Spitfire was faster and more powerful... but the two Mudrys were far ahead of her.

It's too far. I won't be able to catch them.

Connie pushed the Spitfire as hard as she dared, but she knew it wasn't going to be enough. Her instinctive, finely-honed ability to judge distances and speeds told her that it was hopeless.

Unless they both make a mistake on the final corner...

Unfortunately, that didn't look likely. Both planes were piloted by expert racers. One of the planes, a bright canary yellow with white trim, she recognized as belonging to the winner of last year's Rydon Cup. So far he'd flown a careful, flawless course. The other plane, a cerulean blue, was unfamiliar to her, but its pilot clearly had a lot of experience and absolutely no fear. Connie had come perilously close to slamming straight into him earlier, halfway through the race. Her reflexes had saved them both from a mid-air collision, but she'd lost a lot of time straightening out and getting back under control.

Now she could only watch helplessly as the other two planes jostled with each other for first position. The blue daredevil kept trying to cut into the yellow plane's airspace, trying to force it to drop back. Unlike Connie, the pilot of the yellow plane held his nerve, refusing to cede the racing line to the maniac.

They were approaching the final turn point—the infamous hairpin, a true test of a pilot's ability and daring. Connie was certain that the yellow plane would choose to circle wide, taking the turn slowly but safely. She was equally sure the blue plane would attempt the faster but much more dangerous hairpin maneuver, taking the turn as tightly as possible.

If the pilot of the blue plane pulled it off, he'd win the race. If he stalled out, the victory would go to the yellow plane.

Either way, Connie had lost.

I've lost.

I've lost my mother's plane.

I've lost everything.

An alarming, high-pitched whistle shrieked in warning over the deeper snarl of the Spitfire's overheated engine. Her heart like lead in her chest, Connie eased the throttle back a little. There was no sense destroying Chase's plane, even if it was shortly to become Sammy's plane.

A flicker caught her eye, off her left wingtip. Connie craned her neck, hoping against hope that it was Chase. She'd only seen the midnight-black pegasus once, when suddenly he'd shot down past her like the wrath of God, presumably chasing the wyvern.

All through the race, she'd been half-sick with fear for him. She'd clung to the thought that as long as she was still flying without interference from the wyvern, he *had* to be all right, but it was small comfort. If the wyvern wasn't attacking her, it was only because it was attacking *him*.

Now, however, that impossibly winged, glorious equine shape

settled into formation with her. The pegasus was clearly exhausted, but he still kept pace with the plane.

"Chase," Connie breathed, relief filling her.

She couldn't see any wounds on him, though from the stiff way he moved she suspected he was bruised and battered from the fight. She could only assume that the wyvern was worse off, though. Chase must have either killed it or driven it away.

Catching her eye, the pegasus flicked an ear at her. Then he stretched his neck out, his labored wingbeats speeding up so that he inched a little ahead of her. He glanced back at her, tail held high and challenging.

She could read his body language as clearly as if he was speaking directly into her ear: *Well? What are you waiting for?*

Connie set her jaw in determination. If she was going to lose, than she was at least going to go down fighting. She could only pray that she wouldn't *literally* be going down fighting as she gave the plane full throttle once again.

She could feel the stress on the engine in every judder and jerk of the plane underneath her, but this time she held her nerve. The Spitfire howled in fury as it shot across the sky after the two leaders, eating up the distance.

Out of the corner of her eye, she could see Chase struggling gamely to keep up, but she didn't have any attention to spare for him now. All her focus was on holding the plane together, and keeping it true on course. At this speed, the tiniest error could send her tumbling out of control, and out of the race.

Ahead, the two Mudrys had reached the final turn point, the yellow plane still a little ahead of the blue. As she'd suspected, the more experience pilot in the yellow plane began to bank right, describing a wide, looping circle. The more daring blue plane took the opportunity to dash past it. It banked left, so hard that its wings were nearly vertical, trying to complete the turn ahead of the yellow plane.

Even before the blue plane started its turn, Connie knew in her gut that the pilot had come in too hard, too fast. The blue plane stalled, spiraling out of the air. To her relief, he managed to pull back up safely, but he'd plummeted well past the race boundaries. He was out.

The yellow plane had nearly completed the turn. Connie was almost at the turn point herself, but she still had to complete her own loop. By the time she was even facing the finish line, the yellow plane would already have crossed it.

Unless... I attempt the hairpin.

Connie bit her lip hard enough to draw blood. She had only a few heartbeats in which to make the decision.

I can't. It's too dangerous. If it goes wrong, it'll tear the plane apart.

Time seemed to stretch like taffy, seconds slowing to a crawl. She glanced back at Chase, still grimly struggling in her slipstream. Her eyes locked with his, despite the growing distance between them. In that moment, she could *feel* his perfect trust in her, his encouragement and support.

If it goes wrong...

She knew, down to her very bones, that he would catch her.

Connie slammed the control column over.

The Spitfire heeled over on one wingtip, the other pointing up to the sky, metal shrieking with the stress. Connie sucked in her stomach, her visioning threatening to go black as the incredible g-forces squashed her into the pilot's seat. She braced herself with her feet, every muscle in her body straining as she fought to keep control of the plane.

The Spitfire whipped round the hairpin like a comet. The yellow plane's wings see-sawed, buffeted by her wake as Connie's plane screamed past mere feet in front of its nose.

The home stretch lay open before Connie, the clear blue sky wide and welcoming.

She couldn't have slowed the Spitfire down even if she'd wanted to. In mere moments, she was back over land, hurtling toward the airfield. The other plane was just a yellow dot in the distance. Even Chase had fallen away behind her. The crowds below were just a blur of color as she shot over their heads.

Across the finish line.

CHAPTER 18

"We won," Connie said yet again, gazing in disbelief at the Rydon Cup. She hadn't put the massive silver trophy down once since Sammy had been forced to grudgingly present it to her. "We *won*."

"You won," Chase corrected, as he rummaged around in her fridge. He couldn't stop grinning. "You're the one who did the hard work. We just made sure the wyvern didn't get in the way. Right, Killian?"

"Hm?" Killian glanced up from his phone. He'd been rather distracted all the way through the awards ceremony. "Oh. Yes. Definitely."

"Come on, put that thing away. You can't have accumulated that many pressing business emails in a single afternoon." Chase pulled out a magnum of champagne, brandishing it at them both. "We have some serious celebrating to do!"

Connie blinked at the enormous bottle. "When did you sneak that in here? Come to that, how did you even fit it into my fridge?"

"If there's one thing I'm good at," Chase said as he unpeeled the foil, "it's getting oversized things into tight places. As you know."

He was rewarded by the faint flush that crept up Connie's cheeks.

"No, if there's one thing you're good at it's jumping the gun. What would you have done with that thing if we hadn't won?"

Chase hefted the magnum, swinging it experimentally. "Well, I suppose I could have clubbed Sammy to death with the empty bottle, after we'd drowned our sorrows. I hadn't really thought about it. I knew you'd win."

Connie rolled her eyes at him, though a smile pulled at her full lips. "You are *impossible*. Don't shake it up like that, you idiot, or you won't be able to pour it."

"Oh, this one's not for pouring," Chase said cheerfully.

Aiming the bottle at her, he popped the cork. Connie shrieked, holding the Rydon Cup up in defense as he gleefully sprayed her with champagne. For good measure, he blasted Killian too. His cousin swore, hastily shielding his cellphone.

"*Chase!*" Laughing, Connie flicked her dripping hair out of her face. Her eyes sparkled, finally free of all worry and fear. Privately, Chase vowed to shower her in champagne *every* day, if it made her smile like that. "What a waste of good booze."

Holding the still-foaming bottle out to one side, Chase slipped his other arm around her. "I didn't say I was going to let it go to waste."

Regardless of the Rydon Cup digging into his abdomen, he drew her close. He dropped his head to delicately lick a drop of champagne from her neck. Connie's breath hitched as he followed the crisp, fragrant trail up her neck.

The silver trophy trapped between the two of them warmed, absorbing the heat of their bodies. He flicked his tongue teasingly against her soft lips. They parted willingly for him, allowing him to explore her warm mouth. The sweetness of her kiss was more intoxicating than the champagne.

Killian cleared his throat uncomfortably. "Did you say there was another bottle of that?"

Chase could have happily murdered his cousin as Connie jerked away from him, blushing. "Uh, sorry. Um. Yes, we should all celebrate. Together." She looked down at her wet flight suit, which was clinging to her erect nipples, and her blush deepened. "I'm just going to go shower and put on some dry things."

Don't you have some spreadsheets to fill in or something? Chase telepathically snapped at his cousin, as Connie disappeared into the bedroom.

Killian spread his hands apologetically. *Sorry, but I don't think it's a good idea to leave you alone right now. Sammy is probably in a blood-frenzy of rage tonight, and the wyvern is still out there. I want to watch your back until we know everything's blown over.*

Chase knew his cousin was only acting out of concern for his safety. His pegasus still itched to kick Killian over the horizon. *Killian, in the nicest possible way... fuck off. I'll be fine, trust—*

A loud ringing sound made them both jump. Killian stared in confusion at his silent phone for a moment, then shrugged. "Not mine. You?"

Chase had forgotten he was carrying his work cellphone. He was so accustomed to having to be on call, he'd absent-mindedly picked it up that morning even though he'd resigned from being a firefighter. Now he rummaged in his pocket, pulling it out. "Griff? What's up?"

"We're at an incident up in Falmer." Griff's thickened Scottish burr betrayed his concern. "An abandoned apartment block, right at the edge of the city. We think squatters must have accidentally set fire to the place. The caller said she was trapped inside, but Ash and Dai have been in there for ten minutes now and they still haven't found her. It's a real mess in there."

"Shit." In the background, Chase could hear the familiar sing-song shriek of the fire engine. "Hang on, what are you doing on site instead of in the control room?"

"Pretending to be you," Griff said, a touch acidly. "I know you said you were quitting, but Commander Ash hasn't put the paperwork in yet, hoping that you'll change your mind. I volunteered to cover your shift."

"You're on active duty again?" Chase had missed Griff's solid, reliable presence on the team. It had never been quite the same without him.

"Not officially. It's just one of my better days. I can drive a truck, at least. But I can't find people, not like you can. Chase, we really need you."

Chase's first instinct was to leap out the window, to shift and head for the scene at full speed. Nonetheless, he hesitated, glancing at Connie's closed bedroom door. He could hear the shower running in the bathroom.

Go, Killian sent to him, obviously having overheard the conversation thanks to his sharp shifter senses. *You're needed. Don't worry about Connie. I'll tell her where you've gone. And if there's any sign of danger, I'll get her to safety.*

Chase made up his mind. Though it tore at him to leave, there was a life at risk. Connie would understand.

"I'm on my way," he said into the phone.

CHAPTER 19

"Where's Chase?" Connie asked as she came back into the living room.

Killian was on his phone again, thumbing in a text message. "He said he had to dash off," he said, slipping it back into his pocket. "He just jumped out the window and flew away."

"Oh." Connie opened the fridge to look for the second bottle of champagne, hiding her expression.

He probably got some ridiculous idea and had to act on it immediately, she told herself, trying to overcome the sinking feeling of disappointment in her stomach. *He's so impulsive. No doubt he couldn't wait for even a minute.*

...Not even to tell me why he was leaving?

"Did he say when he'd be back?" Connie said, trying to keep her voice light.

"No." Killian touched her arm, making her jump. She hadn't heard him coming up behind her. "Connie, can I ask you something?"

"Sure." She handed him the champagne, and started hunting for wine glasses. "What's on your mind? You've been kind of quiet ever since the race."

Killian turned the bottle in his strong, long-fingered hands, so

129

similar to Chase's. It was strange how two people so physically alike could be so different. "Are you intending to stay with my cousin?"

Connie paused in opening a cupboard.

The race is over. My plane is safe.

I could go anywhere.

"I mean, you won the bet," Killian said, when she didn't say anything. "You don't need him anymore. I love him dearly, but even I have to admit that he's a challenging person to handle. He's reckless, and ridiculous, and just generally..." Killian trailed off, apparently searching for the right adjective.

"Infuriating?" Connie suggested.

"Right." Killian shot her a wry grimace of shared pain. "And God knows, he's hurt you enough in the past. Any sensible person would never want anything to do with him, ever again."

"Yes," Connie said slowly, leaning back against the work surface next to him. She couldn't deny the truth in anything Killian had said. "I guess a sensible person wouldn't."

Killian gestured at her with the wine bottle. "I think you're the most sensible person I've ever met, Connie. You're basically his complete opposite. To be frank, I still can't believe you two are actually meant to be mates. So are you going to stay with him? Despite everything?"

Am I?

Connie searched the clear-eyed, wary, innermost heart of her soul... and knew the answer.

"You know," she said softly. "Ever since my mother died, I've always *had* to be the sensible one. I had to learn to be cautious, to balance my dad. He could afford to be wild and bold, because I would always be there to fix things if it all went wrong. But if *I* was reckless, and it didn't work out... there would be no one to catch *me*."

"But you were reckless today," Killian said.

"Because I knew I could trust Chase to be there if I fell." A slow smile spread across her face. "And I think I'm finally ready to take another risk."

Killian looked at her, his expression unreadable. "So you'll stay with him."

"Yes." Connie patted his tense arm. "Don't worry, Killian. You won't be picking up the pieces of his broken heart this time."

Killian let out his breath in a long sigh. "That's what I was afraid of."

"What?" Connie stared at him, surprised. "I thought you liked me!"

"I do like you," Killian said. There was a strangely regretful expression on his handsome face. "I truly do. You're smart and responsible and much too good for my fool cousin. I wish you would reconsider staying with him. Are you sure I can't persuade you to just disappear? I can give you money, enough to go wherever you want. All you have to do is promise never to let Chase find you, ever again."

"I don't understand," Connie said blankly. "Why do you want me to leave Chase?"

"Because you're a good influence on him." Killian put down the champagne bottle, straightening as if he'd come to a decision. "Too good. I love Chase, I truly do… but I need him to be his worst self. Wild and irresponsible and completely uninterested in the business."

"This is about your *job*?" Connie still couldn't believe what was happening.

"I've worked too hard for too long to lose my place to Chase now." Killian's gray eyes hardened like ice. "*I* am going to be the next CEO of Tiernach Enterprises. Not him."

I'm in danger.

The thought finally percolated through her stunned mind. Heart hammering, Connie tried to make a dash for the door, but Killian was too fast for her. He caught her wrist with inhuman strength, easily restraining her.

"I truly am sorry about this," Killian said, sounding genuinely regretful. "I wish I could have just put you off him again, like I did three years ago. I want you to know, Chase never did cheat on you. I drugged him unconscious, and hired strippers to pretend that he'd slept with him. I staged the whole scene to give you the worst possible impression when you walked in on him. I had to do whatever it took to make you go away. And now, I'm afraid, I have to make sure you go away again. For good, this time."

Someone hammered on the door.

"Help!" Connie yelled, praying that it was Chase.

It wasn't.

"Well now," drawled Sammy, ducking through the doorway. There was nothing either friendly or human about his wide, white smile. "Mighty nice to see you again, Ms. West."

CHAPTER 20

Chase's wings were still sore from fighting the wyvern. It took him an embarrassingly long time to reach the site of the fire. He hardly needed to use his pegasus senses to guide him to his fire team; the orange glow of the fire lit up the horizon, clearly visible for miles.

A thick column of smoke billowed from a derelict apartment block, orange flames roaring out of its shattered windows. Hot air rising from the inferno ruffled his feathers as he spiraled down.

Griff was standing by the fire engine, well back from the blaze. The dispatcher's rugged face was lined with barely-controlled pain, but his fists still clenched as he stared at the fire with helpless frustration. He glanced up as Chase landed, clicking off his radio.

"Am I glad to see you," he said. "Can you sense anyone?"

Quickly shifting back to human form, Chase concentrated. He immediately sensed Commander Ash and Dai, searching through the first floor of the building. He questing out further, searching for any other people inside.

Ignore that. There's no one in there. His pegasus tugged at his attention, trying to drag him toward a nearby alley. *Quick! Kill, strike, hurry!*

Confused by his stallion's agitation, Chase turned his attention in that direction... and stiffened.

There wasn't any in the building, but there *was* someone nearby, watching them all.

Someone he recognized.

"Chase?" Griff said in confusion, but he was already running, leaving the dispatcher behind. With no time to shift, he sprinted for the alleyway as fast as mere human legs could carry him.

DAI! ASH! Chase roared psychically at his colleagues. *Get out here! It's the wyvern!*

He caught sight of a dim silhouette lurking in the shadows the mouth of the alleyway. The small figure hesitated as he ran towards it, then broke and fled—but too late.

With a last burst of speed, Chase hurled himself at the retreating figure. His shoulder connected hard with a soft, yielding form, and the wyvern shifter let out a high-pitched yelp of pain. The impact knocked both of them off their feet. Before the other shifter could recover, Chase threw himself down on top of—her?

"Get off me!" The woman writhed underneath him, her short, plump body no match for his much heavier bulk. "Get off!"

He expected her to shift into her wyvern form, but instead she just grabbed at his wrists with her bare hands. Instantly, a burning pain shot through his skin. Chase swore, involuntarily jerking away from her acidic touch.

The wyvern shifter took advantage of his instinctive recoil to wriggle away from him, rolling to her feet. She turned to flee—

And was stopped dead by a crimson wall of scaled muscle blocking her path. The red dragon growled at her in warning, his enormous bulk filling the alley.

"Thanks, Dai." Chase got to his own feet. He glared at the wyvern shifter. "Don't even think about shifting. You aren't going anywhere."

The woman lifted her chin, matching his glare defiantly. She was dressed in an eclectic mix of ripped black leather and PVC, and had an asymmetric haircut with a thick green stripe dyed into the front. "Bite me, pony-boy," she spat at him. "We both know I can outfly you any day of the week. If I didn't want to be here, I'd already be gone."

His pegasus raged, demanding to trample the wyvern shifter, but he reined his stallion back. Despite her aggressive attitude, there was something vulnerable about her yellow-green eyes and soft, round face. She wore her punkish outfit as if it was a carefully-constructed suit of armor, a way to protect herself from the world rather than an expression of her true self.

Nonetheless, Chase stayed poised on the balls of his feet, ready to grab her if she made any sudden moves. "What *are* you doing here? Did you start this fire?"

"My employer ordered me to." The wyvern shifter folded her tattooed arms, setting her jaw. "But he doesn't know I'm still here. I stayed because I want to talk to your boss."

"If that is so, you have found him," said Ash's calm, cool voice. "I am the Phoenix."

Dai moved back a little to allow the Fire Commander past. Ash looked as composed as ever, but his feet left black, scorched footprints in his wake. Griff followed him, his sharp golden eyes narrowing as they fixed on the wyvern.

Commander Ash stopped in front of the wyvern shifter, his hands clasped behind his back. "What is your name?"

"Ivy," the wyvern shifter said, flinching a little as she met the Commander's calm gaze. "Ivy Viverna."

"Ms. Viverna, you have already committed crimes that call for judgment before the Parliament of Shifters," Ash said. Even from several feet away, Chase could feel the heat radiating from the Commander's motionless form. "But if you have truly committed arson, then you are under my jurisdiction, and subject to *my* judgment. Do you understand?"

"Some shark shifters tried to scare me into surrendering to them, by telling me that it would be much worse if *you* caught me." Ivy hugged herself, her body language an odd combination of fear and determination. "They said you can burn anything. Even a shifter's inner animal."

Commander Ash inclined his head in silent confirmation.

Ivy's lower lip started to tremble. "Can—can you burn away my wyvern?"

Ash considered her for a long moment. "I could. But why would you wish that?"

"I can't touch anyone." Ivy held up her bare hands. Chase's own wrists still burned an angry red where she'd briefly grabbed him. "I'm poisonous, all the time, even in human form. I just want to be normal."

"If I burned your wyvern, you would be an ordinary human," Ash said dispassionately. "But you would not be the same person."

"I don't care." Tears welled up in Ivy's eyes. "I'd rather be anyone else but me. I can't have a regular job. I sell my poisons on the black market, but sometimes even that isn't enough. Then I have to take dirty money for dirty work, or else my little sister doesn't eat, and, and I've never even held her hand! I don't want to live like this any more."

"She's telling the truth," Griff said softly, his golden eyes compassionate.

"Wait," Chase said suddenly, something about what she'd said earlier nagging at him. "What do you mean, some shark shifters came after you?"

"They said their boss was pissed because I damaged his plane." Ivy swiped her sleeve across her eyes. The PVC hissed where her tears touched, acid eating pits into the shiny black material. "I don't know anything about that. My employer just told me to make sure I killed the pilot. He didn't care about the plane."

"*Connie.*" Red rage misted Chase's vision. He would have gone for the wyvern shifter, but Ash flung out an arm to block him. "You tried to kill *my mate.*"

"I'm not an assassin," Ivy flared up, her own fists clenching. "I took the money, but I only ever meant to make the plane crash. I tried to do it slowly enough that the pilot would be able to bail out safely, once they realized what was happening. I didn't want to hurt anyone!"

Chase glanced at Griff, who shrugged. "Still telling the truth."

Chase stared hard at Ivy. "So if you're not working for Sammy Smiles, who *are* you working for?"

Ivy shook her head. "I don't know. I've worked for him for years—selling poisons for him to use against his rivals, mainly. Not to kill them! Just, just little doses, enough to take them out of action for a while, when he needed them out of the way." She didn't meet any of their eyes, shame clear in her young face. "Anyway, he's always been very, very careful not to let me find out who he is."

"Who else would want your mate dead?" Griff asked Chase.

"I don't know, but when I find out *they'll* be dead," Chase growled. "Ivy, if you want to have any *chance* of not spending the rest of your life behind bars, you'd better tell me everything you know about this employer of yours. *Now.*"

Ivy flinched a little, her back pressing against the wall of the alley. "I—I don't know much. He normally texts me with what he wants, but occasionally he mindspeaks to me, so I know he's got to be some sort of mythic shifter. Um. I know he's rich. Oh, and he's got a thing about pegasus shifters."

"You mean he hates us?" Chase tried to think if anyone could want *him* dead. The list was, he had to admit, potentially quite long.

"No, the opposite. He was very clear on this job that I mustn't harm any pegasus shifters." Ivy glared at him, rubbing her side absently. "Clearly you didn't know that, though. You should thank me, Rainbow Dash. It's pretty hard to hold back when someone's trying to kick your ribs in."

Chase furrowed his brow, trying to make the pieces fit together. He had a nagging sense that it should be obvious, that he just wasn't seeing something...

"Ivy," he said slowly. "Did you say that your employer told you to start this fire?"

CHAPTER 21

Connie fought with all her strength, but Killian easily restrained her as Sammy strolled into the room. The shark shifter was followed by a lean, cold-eyed man, clearly one of his thugs.

Connie filled her lungs and screamed as loud as she could, desperately hoping to attract the attention of someone in the neighboring apartments. She only got off one yell, though, before Sammy's henchman slapped a calloused hand over her mouth.

"I'm afraid there's no one nearby to hear you," Killian told her, stepping back as Sammy's man took over the job of restraining her. The pegasus shifter turned to Sammy, frowning. "I thought you were just going to send someone. If anyone asks me if you were here—"

"Now, why would they have any reason to do that?" Sammy replied. He kept his hands in his suit pockets, being careful not to touch anything. "Just wanted to make sure the job was done properly."

Killian jerked his chin at the henchman. "You're positive no one will be able to recognize him?"

"See, that's the nice thing about working with undersea types." Sammy's sharp smile flashed. "A lot of us hardly ever come up on land. Makes it real easy to find someone for this sort of quiet work."

"Good." Killian looked at the henchman. "Tell me you're a wyvern shifter. Out loud."

"I'm a... wyvern shifter?" the thug said, baffled.

"That'll do." The pegasus shifter took a small, sheathed knife out of his pocket. "I need to be able to say that I thought you were one. We're ready, then."

Killian unsheathed the knife. It was only a small blade, but Killian handled it as gingerly as if it was a loaded gun. The edge of the steel looked corroded, and was coated in some thick, oily fluid.

Killian held the handle in the tips of his fingers, offering it to Sammy's henchman. The man glanced at it, then looked questioningly at Sammy.

The shark shifter rocked a little on the balls of his feet. "Now, I can't tell you what to do, son. But I will just say that the little lady here has been a mighty sharp thorn in my side. Not that I'd ever want anyone to hurt her seriously, mind."

With a shrug, Sammy's henchman took the proffered knife in one hand, still restraining Connie with his other arm. Connie tried to cringe away from the blade, but even one-handed, the thug easily held her motionless.

With a quick, practiced flick, he drew the sharp edge across her cheek.

It happened so fast that Connie didn't even feel any pain. Then she realized that she couldn't feel *anything*. The absolute numbness spread out from the cut and across her face, terrifyingly fast.

"I hope it doesn't hurt," Killian said to her, in genuine concern. "I specifically told my wyvern to make me a poison that wouldn't hurt. I don't want you to suffer, Connie."

"You... won't... get away," Connie forced out around her numb tongue. "Chase..."

"Will never know the truth," Killian finished for her, calmly. He held his arms outspread, cocking his head at Sammy's henchman. "I need to be able to truthfully say that I tried to fight you off. Please, make it look good."

Connie collapsed helplessly to the floor as the man released her.

She could only watch, paralysis spreading through every muscle of her body, as Sammy's thug delivered a swift, thorough beating to Killian.

Chase, she thought desperately.

She remembered Ash saying that mythic shifters were telepathic. Chase was her mate. Would he be able to sense her distress?

CHASE! she called out mentally, praying that he could hear her. Praying that he was on his way.

"Enough," Killian gasped after a few brutal minutes. He held up a hand. "That'll do."

The henchman glanced at Sammy, who lifted one finger, scratching his nose. The henchman swiveled on one foot, swinging one last blow straight at Killian's face. The pegasus shifter cried out, hunching over.

"*That* was for sending my plane to the bottom of the sea," Sammy said, his smile cruel and savage. "It's going to cost me a pretty penny to get it fixed up. You sure your cousin isn't going to notice that it's gone?"

"I'll handle that." Killian straightened again, blood streaming from his broken nose. "He'll be too devastated over losing his mate to care about anything else."

"You better see that you do." Sammy glanced at his henchman, his black eyes cold. "Just one last thing to do, then."

"Boss?" His thug looked confused.

He never saw the pegasus's hooves coming.

"There," Killian said, shifting back again. "Now I can say that the wyvern shifter broke in here and I killed him, but not before he managed to poison Connie. Even if Chase calls in his truth-teller friend, the story will check out. You should go now."

"Not yet." Sammy crouched down on his heels next to Connie, staring intently into her face. "No one crosses me and lives to boast about it. I want to see the light go out of her eyes."

Chase...

Her vision was going dark. The last thing she saw was Sammy's sharp, triumphant smile.

CHAPTER 22

Chase...

Even though they weren't fully bonded, Chase could feel Connie calling his name. Her faint mental voice was growing weaker by the second.

Chase flew as he'd never flown before. All the aches and pains of his battered body fell away, as nothing compared to the overwhelming need to get to Connie. He flashed across the night sky like a shooting star, not even bothering to make himself invisible. His mate needed him now, *now!*

...Chase...

Even as he arrowed down toward her apartment building, her psychic call faded away into silence. Terror filled his heart. There was no time to land, no time to shift. He folded his wings as tightly as he could, aiming straight at her window.

He burst through in a shower of glass and splinters, taking the entire window and a good deal of the wall with him. Even in the chaos of flying debris, he knew with crystal clarity exactly where Connie was. She lay prone on the floor, barely breathing, Sammy Smiles crouched over her like a vulture.

He tucked up his hooves, leaping Connie's limp form as he

knocked the shark shifter away from her. Sammy went flying, smashing hard into the far wall. Sammy bared his teeth, his form starting to swell into a monstrous shark-headed shape—but Chase whirled, kicking him hard in the chest with both back hooves. Sammy went down, and this time, he didn't get up again.

"Chase," Killian gasped. His cousin staggered forward, hand outstretched, his face a mask of blood. "Thank God. Sammy brought—"

LIAR! Chase slammed into him. Killian gasped as a thousand pounds of angry equine crushed him into the corner. *You hired the wyvern! You tried to kill my mate! YOU!*

"I—I would never have hurt you." Killian's eyes swiveled, searching for any way to escape, but Chase had him boxed in with no room to shift. "Just calm down and I'll explain. You don't want to hurt me either, not really. I'm your cousin!"

Not kin. Chase's stallion laid its ears flat back against its skull. *Rival!*

Chase reared over his cousin, his iron-hard hooves directly over Killian's head. It would be so easy...

Too easy.

He flicked out one foreleg, clipping Killian neatly on the side of the head. His cousin collapsed, knocked out cold.

Kill! urged his stallion.

No, Chase told his pegasus, turning away. *He hurt our mate. He must lose everything, as he sought to take everything from us. He will never fly again, never run again, never be free again. He will live the rest of his life behind bars, and every day, every minute of his wretched existence, he will know that* he *lost.*

Chase heard the sing-song wail of an approaching siren. Griff's friends in the police were on their way. There was no time to wait for them, though. He could feel Connie's faltering pulse as if her heart beat inside his own chest.

Chase seized Connie's collar in his teeth, awkwardly jerking his head round to sling her across his broad back. She hung limp, arms and legs dangling down. As soon as he had her secure, Chase launched himself out the hole in the wall as smoothly as he could, soaring back up into the cool night air.

HUGH! he sent telepathically, his pegasus senses reaching out to find the paramedic. *I need you, NOW!*

I'm at a traffic incident. Hugh's mental voice was as terse and clipped as his physical one. *I'm a little busy—*

I'm bringing Connie to you. He wheeled round, locking onto the paramedic's location. *I think she's been poisoned by wyvern venom.*

Hugh swore, the mental picture bright and profane. *Then you'd better get here fast.*

Chase flew as quickly as he dared. Every slight slip of Connie's body across his back made his heart leap into his mouth. He kept having to twitch one way or the other to keep her from sliding off.

Fortunately, Hugh wasn't far away. In mere minutes, Chase caught sight of the paramedic's distinctive white hair. Hugh was standing some way back from a couple of smoking, smashed cars piled up at the side of the road. John Doe was there, too, wielding a hose to put out the flaming vehicles—and no doubt surreptitiously using his sea dragon ability to control water to assist the process.

"You're in luck," Hugh said as Chase touched down next to him. The paramedic was cleaning blood off his bare hands with an antiseptic wipe. "I just sent off the ambulance with the casualties. Let's see her, then."

Chase shifted, catching Connie in his arms as he did so. He lowered her to the ground, stepping back to allow Hugh access. The paramedic crouched over her, his face going intent and focused as he ran his long fingers over her skin. His breath hissed out between his teeth.

"Close your eyes," Hugh demanded abruptly.

"What?" Chase stared at him, taken aback. "Why?"

"Because I have to shift to heal her." Hugh shot a quick glance at John Doe, but the sea dragon shifter already had his back to them, fully occupied with the car fire. The paramedic looked back at Chase, scowling fiercely. "If you want me to save your mate, then close your Goddamn eyes!"

Chase would have happily plucked out his own eyes, if it would save Connie. He squeezed them shut as tight as he could, desperately praying as he did so.

Please. Please let this work...

A soft, silvery light shone through his closed eyelids. A faint, elusive fragrance filled the air, like lilacs after rain. Everything seemed to go very still and quiet. All of his aches and bruises faded away, washed clean by that subtle, healing radiance.

What's this? His pegasus pricked up its ears, nostrils flaring as if catching wind of a familiar scent. *Kin?*

Hush. Chase kept his eyes scrunched shut, not daring to risk distracting Hugh from his task. Privately, he swore he would never, ever again tease Hugh for his mysterious ways, if only he could heal Connie now.

The light faded. "There," Hugh said, sounding exhausted but satisfied.

"Connie!" Chase flung himself down next to her. He cradled her as she drew in a deep, hacking breath.

"She's stable now, but she'll still need fluids and rest." Hugh rose, pulling his customary surgical gloves back on. "I'm going to call an ambulance."

Chase stroked Connie's hair back from her white face. "I'm here, Connie. I've got you. Everything's going to be okay."

Her eyes fluttered open. They fixed on him, widening.

"Chase," she said, joy and love shining from her face. She nestled against his chest, leaning on him with perfect trust. "Yes."

EPILOGUE

One Week Later

"Are you peeking?" Chase demanded.

"I'm not, I promise!" Giggling, Connie clung to his neck, the blindfold over her face tickling her nose with every step Chase took. "But I swear I will, if you don't put me down soon. When you said you had a surprise, I thought you meant close by!"

"Nearly there," Chase promised, which was what he'd said five minutes ago, when he'd swept her up in his arms, and fifteen minutes before *that*, during the car ride from the hospital. Connie was starting to wonder if the next stage of the mysterious journey was going to involve a charter jet. She wouldn't put it past him.

This time, however, it seemed that they really were nearly there. Connie felt him fumble in his pocket, and heard a beep followed by a louder rumbling that sounded like a vast garage door sliding open. After a moment, the noise stopped, and Chase finally set her down on her feet again.

"I couldn't find a 'Glad You've Finally Fully Recovered from Being

Poisoned By A Wyvern' card," Chase said as he untied the silk blindfold from around her head. "Hallmark seem to have overlooked that opportunity, strangely. So I got you a present instead."

Connie blinked, briefly dazzled by the bright lights after having had her eyes closed for so long. For a second, she just had a vague impression of a large, gleaming, olive-green blur in front of her...

"Oh," she gasped, as her vision came clear. "*Oh.*"

The Spitfire listed a little, propped up by scaffolding on one side where the left wheel assembly had been torn away. There were great, crumpled gashes in the plane's underbelly, and both cockpits were completely smashed. The propeller was bent and twisted.

But it was hers.

Her Spitfire.

Her mother's plane.

"I know it looks a mess," Chase said anxiously, as she drifted dreamlike toward the Spitfire. "But John spent ages searching the sea floor, and he swears on the honor of his people that he found all the parts. I've dried everything out and cleaned it as best I could, but I don't know how to fix it myself and I didn't trust anyone else to work on it without your approval. I promise, we'll get her restored, no matter what. You can have whatever you need to repair it, or I could hire specialists, or, or... Connie?"

Gently, as if the Spitfire might bolt away like a startled deer if she moved too fast, Connie laid her hand flat on the plane's battered surface.

"Hello again, baby," she whispered.

Chase let out his breath in a long sigh of relief. "So she's okay?"

"She's *perfect.*" Connie stroked the plane, blinking back tears at being able to touch it again. "It'll take some time, but I'll make her good as new. It'll be like... it'll be like working with my mother. Fixing the same things that she fixed, all those years ago."

He came up behind her, softly resting his hands on her shoulders. "I think she would have liked that. She'd be very proud of you." A slightly pained note crept into his voice. "I'd say she'd be even prouder than your dad is, but I'm not sure that's humanly possible."

Connie giggled, leaning back against his broad chest. "So I guess he must have subjected you to the story of how I won the Rydon Cup in a borrowed rustbucket, while flying backward and upside-down."

"Twice. I *did* try to remind him that I was actually there, but he kept talking anyway." Chase sounded aggrieved. "I wish I could tell him what really happened. My version of the story is much better."

"Serves you right, having to hold your tongue while someone else prattles on for once." Connie bit her lip. "Um. While we're talking planes... I have a confession to make. About your Spitfire."

"It's your Spitfire," Chase said, without hesitation. "Your other Spitfire. I'm not letting you give it back."

"Good, because I kind of can't." Connie tilted her head to look up at him. "I traded it to my dad. He can race it, display it, sell it, whatever he wants... but it'll be on his own. I'm done bailing him out now. I love him, but I can't go through anything like this again."

"You won't," Chase said fiercely, his arms tightening around her. "I promise. I'm glad you're spreading your own wings at last. Your dad has to learn to fly on his own, too."

"Speaking of dads." Connie raised her eyebrows at him. "Did you talk to yours yet?"

"Yes." She felt all his muscles tense. "With Killian in jail, Tiernach Enterprises is in chaos. My father needs to stabilize things as quickly as possible. He's got some potential replacements lined up, but he'd still prefer it if I took over as CFO."

Connie put her hand over his, squeezing it. "Will you?"

He looked down at her, his eyes dark and unreadable. "Do you want me to?"

"I want you to be happy," she said. Her thumb rubbed soothing circles on the back of his hand. "And somehow I don't think sitting behind a desk all day would do that."

He let out a brief, sharp laugh. "No."

Chase fell silent for a long moment, his face shadowed. "He got me into firefighting, did I ever tell you that? Killian, I mean. After you left, all those years ago. I was determined to just blindly charge around the world searching for you, but he persuaded me to leave that to professional detectives. I needed something to keep me busy, so he told me about this all-shifter fire crew he'd heard about. He thought it might suit me."

"He did know you very well," Connie said, softly.

"And it *does* suit me," Chase admitted. Gradually, the tension eased from his body, though he still looked subdued. "I like doing something real, that demands all my mind and strength and skill. I like being able to use my talents to help people. You don't mind if I stick with it? I mean, it's a dangerous job. I wouldn't want you to be constantly worrying about me."

"Chase, I fly vintage WWII warplanes for a living," Connie said, a touch acerbically. "Exactly which one of us should be worrying about the other, again?"

He laughed again, and Connie was pleased that it was his real laugh this time, warm and unrestrained. "You have a point, there." He cocked his head to one side. "Hey. You said you traded your other Spitfire to your dad, but you didn't say what for. What did you get in return?"

Connie patted her Spitfire again. "The other half of this. When my mom died, her will left me and my dad both half-shares in her plane. I used your Spitfire to buy him out. She's all mine now."

"And no one will ever be able to take her away from you again," Chase finished for her, with great satisfaction.

"Well... that's not strictly true." Connie turned in his arms, stepping back a little so that she could meet his eyes properly. "Because I'm giving half of her to you."

Chase's mouth dropped open. "Connie—"

She put a finger on his lips, silencing him. "I know you don't need the money. But I don't want to start off our lives together in debt to you, either. So I'm going to insist on this. She's half yours, and half mine, and that's that."

His face went very still, his eyes wide and dark as he looked into hers. "Our lives together?"

Connie stretched up on her toes to kiss him in answer. His mouth was light and gentle on hers, as if he hardly dared to breathe.

Then his hands came up to softly frame her face. His long, agile fingers caressed her as he deepened the kiss. The sweetness of it sang through Connie's body, until she felt as if his hands were the only thing stopping her from floating up, up into the sky.

"In that case," Chase murmured into her lips, "I have a question for you."

Even though she should really have been used to it by now, Connie's heart still skipped a beat as he went down on one knee.

"Constance West." He took her hand. "Will you be my mate?"

Connie blinked down at him. "Okay, I have to admit, that's not what I was expecting. I thought I already was your mate?"

"You are. But we aren't *mated*. It's... different." He looked like he was struggling to find words to explain it. "There's a sort of ritual that we do. Afterwards, we'd be true, bonded mates."

"Like Virginia and Dai?" Connie asked. She remembered the deep, powerful connection between the dragon shifter and his mate, so strong it was almost visible.

Chase nodded. "We'd be able to talk telepathically, like I do with other mythic shifters. We'd know what each other is feeling, share our deepest desires and needs. We'd be truly joined. Forever."

Connie's breath caught. "Oh, yes. Yes. Let's do it."

She could so clearly see Chase's joy shining in his eyes, it was like their souls were already joined. "Now?"

Connie laughed, feeling wonderfully wild and reckless. "Yes, now! *Can* we? What do we do?"

"There are a couple of steps, to bring us closer together." Chase stood, taking both her hands in his. "First, we fly back to my nest."

"I assume that's not flying in a plane." Connie's pulse sped up at the prospect of riding the pegasus again—partly with excitement, but also with nervousness.

She'd never learned how to ride. As a kid, when most of her friends had been horse-mad, she'd been wallpapering her bedroom with posters of vintage warplanes.

Chase won't let me fall.

"What happens after we get back to your place?" she asked him.

A slow, wicked grin spread across Chase's face, kindling an answering heat low in Connie's belly. "To find *that* out, you'll have to ride me there."

Rising, Chase retreated a few steps. His tall, strong form shimmered. Between one blink and the next, the black pegasus stood before her.

All the breath whooshed out of Connie's lungs. She hadn't had the chance to see him properly like this before. The elegant arch of his strong neck would have put the finest Arabian stallion to shame. But while he had the graceful, lean build of a thoroughbred racehorse, his back was higher than the top of her head. He was the biggest horse she'd ever seen.

Awestruck, she circled him. He stayed still to let her look at him, though his alert ears swiveled to follow her. The lights struck gleaming purple and blue highlights from his folded wings. His sleek black coat held the same iridescence, but subtler. He gleamed as if carved from black opal.

He knelt, stretching out one wing. Heart thudding, Connie scrambled up onto his back. She had to hike up her dress a little to straddle him, his hide warm and soft against her bare thighs. He stayed steady as she tucked her legs under his folded wings.

"Okay," she said, when she felt as secure as she was going to get. Tentatively, she squeezed his sides a little with her legs. "I'm ready."

Chase took a single delicate step forward, and stopped.

"I said I'm ready." She nudged him again, a little harder. "Let's go!"

Chase curved his neck to look back at her, the deep black eye wide and innocent. Then he began to amble toward the door at a pace so sedate, he could have been overtaken by a tortoise.

Connie rolled her own eyes at him. "Don't think I don't know what you're up to. But, if you insist..."

She kicked him hard in the ribs with her heels, like a cowboy in a movie. "Heigh-ho, Silver! Giddy-up!"

Chase snorted with equine laughter. She instinctively grabbed at his silky mane as his huge muscles bunched under his velvet-soft fur.

Then, he *ran*.

Connie shrieked, flinging herself flat against his neck as he went from a standing start to a flat-out gallop in barely a heartbeat. The instant they were clear of the hanger, his wings spread, each reaching primary feathers as long as Connie's entire arm. He leaped, his wings sweeping down as his back hooves left the ground.

It was nothing like flying in a plane. The wind roared all around her, whipping Chase's long black mane into her face as he soared upward. The ground fell away with dizzying speed. Connie clung to him for dear life, her arms wrapped around his neck so tight she worried she might throttle him.

Yet for all his terrifying speed and the lack of any sort of safety harness, he bore her up as smoothly as her own plane. She could feel the constant movement of his muscles, adjusting to match every tiny shift in her own body.

Gradually, Connie's hammering heart began to slow. She dared to sit up a little, squinting against the wind. Brighton spread out beneath them, sunset turning its old, stately buildings to gold. She'd never been able to look straight down while flying before. The whole world spread out at her feet, intricate and inviting.

She laughed out loud in sheer, surprised joy. Chase pranced on thin air, showing his pleasure in her delight.

Greatly daring, Connie let go of his mane. Chase stayed steady as a rock underneath her. Closing her eyes, she spread her arms wide. The wind streamed through her outstretched fingers.

For the first time in her life, she truly knew what it was to *fly*, like a bird, on her own two wings.

Chase tipped one wing down, banking. Connie shifted her weight, knowing from the subtle movements of his muscles under her bare thighs what he was going to do even before he started to spiral downward. She could see Chase's rooftop garden below them. Tiny, glimmering lights marked its edges, guiding them to the landing lawn.

Chase's hooves delicately touched down. He knelt again to allow her to dismount. She slid off his back, feeling a little regretful to feel ground under her feet again.

Laying her cheek against his gleaming hide, she hugged his neck hard. "That was amazing. Part of me wishes we could stay up in the sky forever."

The pegasus's smooth, glossy fur dissolved under her hands—and became warm, human skin. Chase's arms slid round her. "Then I'd better make it worth your while to come down."

Connie gasped, feeling his massive erection pressing against her soft stomach as he pulled her close. His eyes were dark pools of desire. Despite his clear need, he kissed her lightly. Connie closed her eyes, melting against him as he gently explored and tasted her mouth. His teasing tongue sent pleasure racing through her veins, and a surge of wetness between her thighs.

Hungry for more, she tried to deepen the kiss—but his hands closed over her shoulders, holding her back. "Slowly," he said, hoarsely. "This time, we take things slowly. I want to learn every inch of you."

Connie slid her hands over his chest, feeling the hardness of his muscles under the soft cotton shirt. She let her fingers drift lower, popping open the button of his jeans. "Do I get to do the same to you?"

Chase caught his breath as she lightly traced the bulge of his straining cock. "Yes. Oh, *God* yes." He caught her wrist. "Though maybe you shouldn't start there."

Backing off a little, he pulled his shirt over his head. Connie's breath sighed out of her. The fading sunset highlighted the beautiful planes of his torso, every muscle sharp and defined. Framed by lush rosebushes edging the garden, he looked like some classical statue brought to life.

Taking her hands in his, he lay her palms flat against his shoulders, wordlessly inviting her to explore. She slid her hands over his warm skin, hardly able to believe that this Greek god of a man could really be *hers*.

His chest rose sharply as she brushed over his hard nipples. Somehow, she could sense the shock of pleasure that went through him, as if it was echoed in her own body. She could feel how his skin sang to her every touch, how the light scratch of her nails made his desire rise, hot and urgent.

Wanting to see all of him, she pushed his jeans and underwear down over his lean hips. He clenched his fists, his abs knotting as she knelt to pull the rest of his clothes off. She could feel how hard it was for him to hold back, how badly he wanted to touch her.

His hard cock strained above her, thick and full. Even though she knew he wanted to take things slow, Connie couldn't resist tasting him, just a little. His breath exploded out of him as she ran her tongue up the thick shaft. He yanked her up, so hard and fast she nearly overbalanced.

"My turn now," he said, a feral heat burning in his eyes.

As if unable to restrain himself any longer, his strong hands quickly undid the buttons at the front of her dress. He pushed the silky fabric off her shoulders, and Connie wriggled a little so that the dress fell to pool at her feet.

"So beautiful." Chase's hand trembled as he traced the curves of her shoulder, sliding her bra strap off. "My beautiful mate. Let me see you. Let me worship you."

His touch left trails of fire on her skin as he slid her bra off. His light, teasing fingers skimmed her curves, moving down to hook under her panties. Slowly, still looking up at her, Chase knelt, pulling her panties down as he did so. His touch on her thighs was exquisite torture, leaving her breathless with desire for more.

"Connie," Chase growled, a rough catch in his voice betraying his own desire. He pulled her down, catching her in his arms and laying her back on the soft grass. His hands slid up her legs, spreading them wide so that he could kneel between them. "My mate."

Totally exposed before his hungry gaze, the gentle breeze caressing her bare skin, Connie had never felt more beautiful. He looked at her as if she was a miracle, a goddess, everything he could ever want.

Chase dipped his head, planting a trail of kisses up her sensitive inner thigh. Connie moaned, winding her fingers into his hair, trying to urge him on faster. Yet still he held back, taking his time, making her quiver with frustrated lust as he slowly, so slowly worked his way upward.

When his tongue finally traced her wet folds, Connie's hips jerked upward at the electric shock of it. Spreading her wide with his fingers, he licked her firmly, every touch making her writhe and sob with helpless pleasure. That growing connection between them showed him exactly how to circle her, exactly what she needed to reach her peak. She arched up as orgasm rushed over her.

Please, please, more, now!

"Yes," Chase gasped.

Drawing back, he flipped her over. His strong hands on her hips urged her onto her knees, pulling her up against him. His torso pressed against her back as he effortlessly lifted her to exactly the position he wanted. Anticipation sang through Connie's body as his hard cock rubbed against her eager entrance, her juices slicking the swollen head. She'd never felt so ready, so desperate.

With a single hard thrust, he sank fully into her. It was as if he sank into her mind, her very soul, at the same time. His love for her enfolded her even as her body enfolded his. She cried out, lost to everything, everything except him. She matched him thrust for thrust, spiraling up into ecstasy in perfect union.

My mate!

He bit down on the base of her neck as he thrust one last time. The edge of pain made an exquisite counterpoint to her ecstasy, sweeping her over the edge. His fierce satisfaction at marking her filled her, as much as his hot seed did.

She was his now, as he was hers.

Forever.

They collapsed down onto the grass together, breathing as hard as if they'd just run a marathon. Connie felt deliciously exhausted, undone in every muscle.

She snuggled back into Chase, intertwining her fingers through his. "So... are we mated now?"

Oh yes. His voice sounded not in her ears, but inside her head.

Connie twitched in surprise, and Chase laughed. *Very, very thoroughly mated.*

Good, she thought at him, and knew that he'd heard her from the jolt of pleased surprise that he sent back. She wriggled round in his arms to face him. *In that case, I have a question for you.*

Oh? Chase smiled at her, his love enfolding her like strong wings.

She could feel his complete happiness, his awestruck delight that *she* had chosen *him*. She could sense his bone-deep determination to be worthy of her.

Chase Tiernach. Connie looked deep into his warm black eyes. *Will you marry me?*

Printed in Great Britain
by Amazon